A Sense of Belonging

NORTH CAROLINA BOOK 3

A Sense of Belonging

A NOVEL OF ROMANCE NESTLED IN THE HEART OF THE TAR HEEL STATE

Terry Fowler

THORNDIKE PRESS

An imprint of Thomson Gale, a part of The Thomson Corporation

THOMSON
GALE™

Detroit • New York • San Francisco • New Haven, Conn. • Waterville, Maine • London

THOMSON
GALE

Thorndike Press, an imprint of The Gale Group.

Thorndike Press® Large Print Christian Fiction.
The text of this Large Print edition is unabridged.
Other aspects of the book may vary from the original edition.
Set in 16 pt. Plantin.

LIBRARY OF CONGRESS CATALOGING-IN-PUBLICATION DATA

Fowler, Terry (Terry S.)
A sense of belonging : a novel of romance nestled in the heart of the Tar Heel State / by Terry Fowler.
p. cm. — (North Carolina ; bk. 3) (Thorndike Press large print Christian fiction)
ISBN-13: 978-0-7862-9828-0 (hardcover : alk. paper)
ISBN-10: 0-7862-9828-6 (hardcover : alk. paper)
1. Undertakers and undertaking — North Carolina — Fiction. 2. Chief executive officers — Fiction. 3. North Carolina — Fiction. 4. Large type books. I. Title.
PS3556.O86S46 2007
813'.54—dc22 2007024421

Published in 2007 by arrangement with Barbour Publishing, Inc.

Printed in the United States of America on permanent paper
10 9 8 7 6 5 4 3 2 1

In loving memory of my mother, Martha,
who shared my love of the written word
and taught me to persevere.
Special thanks to my sister, Tammy;
my friends, Dianne Abbott,
Darlene Roberts, Trisha Sunholm;
my critique partners, Gail Martin,
Lynn Coleman, Becky Dryden,
Mary Gaskins;
and all the members of the Sea Scribes
for their faith and encouragement.

Chapter 1

Sharley Montgomery closed her eyes and opened them slowly. Yep — there was a helicopter in her parking lot. Just sitting there, precisely parked within the white lines of a parking space, as though the pilot were confused about whether its identity belonged to earth or air.

Sharley felt no confusion. They were miles from the airport, so it had to be a joke. After all, her longtime employees had been struggling for weeks to come up with something to pay her back for the last prank she'd pulled on them. Devlin and Jack must have called in a lot of favors on this one.

Well, too bad. She'd learned the definition of a poker face at her father's knee. Jack and Devlin would crack before she did. She would act as though there was nothing out of the ordinary. That would surely drive them crazy.

Sharley slipped through the back door of

Montgomery-Sloan. The austere surroundings contrasted sharply with the more formal front entrance. Sharley had grown up in these back rooms, watching her father and Uncle Ben, his brother-in-law, perform the tasks others considered morbid.

Jack sat with his feet propped on the ancient government surplus desk, his face hidden behind the few pages that constituted the daily release of the town's newspaper.

Sharley fixed a pleasant smile on her face. "Good morning, Jack."

The paper dropped. "Morning, boss. There's a guy waiting in your office. Flew in on that chopper."

She had to give it to him. He was putting on a good act, better than usual. "Did he say what he wanted?"

Jack shrugged. "Something about finalizing some arrangements."

"I take it he considered your break more important than his business?"

Jack grinned at her dry humor. "I'm not supposed to be here until ten. Besides, he wants to deal directly with the boss."

The boss. No way would she admit that those words always made her want to look for her father. "Thanks, Jack." She headed toward the front and stopped, turning back to add, "When you get here at ten, how about running out to pick up the chairs at the Adams place? Sheila told me her mom's going back to Raleigh with her this afternoon."

"Can do."

Sharley glanced in the mirrored hall tree just outside her office, taking a moment to smooth her hair and put on her serious facade. People had certain expectations of funeral home directors. They needed to be staid, grave, worthy of respect, and blend into their surroundings like one of the knots in fine wood paneling.

Sometimes, because of her appearance, she was hard put to convince them she was a knowledgeable professional. One who had already apprenticed at the hands of the best before obtaining her own training. Her father had done his job well. Sharley knew what needed to be done and prepared to do exactly that as she reached for the door's hand-carved knob.

What was taking so long? Kenan Montgomery's gaze swept toward the door for the hundredth time. Telling Sam about his vacation plans was his first mistake. This year he planned to fly a chopper along the coastline, but when he briefly mentioned the idea to the old man while seeking approval for the time off, the old man made him an offer he couldn't refuse. The company helicopter, all expenses paid, for two weeks with only one stipulation — one little favor. And truth be told, the trip had been a pleasure, Kenan admitted, dragging in a deep breath as he glanced around the tastefully decorated office — up until now.

Kenan tried to trick himself, to pretend he was waiting for one of the up-and-coming young executives he dealt with daily. When that didn't work, he thought about the pleasures of his journey — the beautiful scenery, wild ponies and dolphins at play, and touching down wherever the urge struck. The solitude had given him time for personal reflection, and he decided his life was pretty good. Or at least it was until about thirty minutes ago when he entered the ornate doors of Montgomery-Sloan Funeral Home.

Of all the tasks Sam had ever sent him to perform, this was the strangest. *The most ghoulish. Morbid. Unnatural.* The phrases jumped into his mind with frightening regularity.

Sam had been determined. Kenan's protests did little good, since his eccentric but wealthy employer thought nothing of sending his right-hand man to make advance funeral arrangements for him. The elderly man had bluntly announced he was old and dying and needed to make final arrangements for his burial while he was still alive, to be sure they were exactly as he wanted them.

Kenan argued that it was something best done in person. Sam countered that he wasn't up to the trip. The man ran a multimillion-dollar organization like it was child's play, so that one was a little difficult to swallow. But what could Kenan say? His masculine ego wouldn't let him admit that funeral homes gave him the creeps.

At six, he had attended his first visitation and managed to get himself locked in the funeral home for several hours. After that nightmare-filled evening of his young life, Kenan vowed never to subject himself to such incidents again. He hadn't set foot in a funeral home since, always finding a reason to be elsewhere, sending large, expensive flower arrangements in his stead.

"Then we'll wait until you feel up to it," he told the old man. "Or better yet, you can have Jamie drive you to a local business to make your choices."

"No!" the old man roared, something he did occasionally when he felt the need to exert his authority. "The Montgomery family buried my ancestors, and they'll bury me."

"Fine. We'll fax them information on what you want, and they can submit the plans for your approval," Kenan offered just as decisively.

Sam changed tactics then, fixing pleading eyes on him as his voice turned soft and shaky. "Kenan, do this one last thing for an old man. You're like a son. I trust your choices. There's no one else."

And because he owed Sam so much, Kenan had spent the last few hours dreading his arrival in the little remote North Carolina town. *Remote is the key word,* he thought; he'd had to touch the chopper down in the parking lot because the nearest airport was two hours away.

He couldn't help but wonder about Sam's ties to the area. Kenan knew it was more than a passing acquaintance. After all, the name of the town was Samuels. And though he knew there was no delaying the inevitable and that it was best to just jump on this task and get it over with, Kenan couldn't escape his desire to run and never look back. Why Sam thought it was necessary now was beyond him. The way he had it figured, the peppery old man would be around when Kenan himself was a grandfather.

The man sitting in her visitor's chair was obviously uneasy, Sharley decided. In fact, a corpse in the throes of rigor mortis would probably be more comfortable. Still, that white-blond hair was something else, the shade as light as a small child's before the passing of time darkened its color.

"Hello. Sorry to have kept you waiting."

The man jumped and shot to his feet. "Kenan Montgomery."

Sharley smiled and gestured toward the chair. "Any relation to the local Montgomerys?"

"None that I know of. I was raised in Texas."

"Strange how people can have the same last name and not be related," she mused.

"We're all descendants of Adam and Eve."

"That's true." Sharley swallowed hard as his obsidian eyes touched on her face.

"Then there's always the possibility that we're kissing cousins." She almost laughed when he shifted uneasily, barely managing a feeble smile before he added, "I'm here to make arrangements for my employer's funeral."

Sharley decided Kenan Montgomery was

quite a man. Now that she was closer to him, she realized he was older than she had first thought. Fine lines creased the corners of his eyes and silver glinted in his blond hair. He was six feet tall, with a muscular breadth of shoulders that convinced her he was a weight lifter. His towhead and black eyes were a magnificent contrast to the deeply tanned skin. She jerked her eyes away, then seated herself and reached into the drawer for a folder containing the necessary paperwork.

"Please have a seat. When did your employer pass away?"

"He didn't."

Her head lifted, and she fixed her questioning gaze on him.

"He feels he's getting old and wants the arrangements made in advance," Kenan offered. "He sent me to make them."

"I see." *Stranger and stranger,* Sharley thought and stifled a grin. Just what were the guys up to with this one? A helicopter and a decidedly uncomfortable actor making funeral arrangements for a man who was not dead. She couldn't wait to see how this turned out.

"A number of people prefer making arrangements in advance," she said. "They feel it spares their loved ones the added pain during their time of grief. What does he have in mind?"

Sharley believed in the services her business provided. Every potential customer who stepped through the doors received her undivided attention. She had a drawer full of contracts for people who had planned their services to the minutest detail, some much more flamboyantly than she would have chosen, but it was their funeral. A tiny smile teased her lips at the pun.

"No insult intended, but in this case, I think it would be best if I dealt directly with the owner."

"No offense taken," she murmured. Steepling her hands under her chin, Sharley relaxed and said, "I'm Charlotte Montgomery. Montgomery-Sloan is my business. How can we be of service to you?"

Sharley hid another smile. If his jaw slackened any more, his mouth would be hanging open. An old, familiar feeling hit her, and her smile faded. As a child, she had endured the other kids' taunting. Things had changed little over the years. She had yet to meet the man who could get past her profession.

People still reacted strangely when she told them her occupation. Those were always the most inconvenient times when her rebellious nature struggled with the quiet dignity her profession demanded.

She weighed the situation and decided on business as usual. "If you'll accompany me into the display room, I'll show you our selection of caskets and vaults. Once those decisions are made, it shouldn't take too long to finalize the arrangements."

Gooseflesh chased themselves over Kenan's arms, his stomach feeling as if he'd taken a deep breath and forgotten to release it. *The oxygen deficiency must be messing with my brain,* he thought, as he somehow managed to get to his feet and follow her.

Though she certainly did something for the pencil-thin black skirt she wore with a hand-painted blouse, not even Charlotte Montgomery's feminine sway could take his mind off the pending event. He couldn't believe this beautiful woman was a mortician. His first impression had been she was totally out of place, not belonging to the macabre profession.

"The markers are in the corners. Please feel free to look around. I'll be in the office if you have any questions."

Sales psychology is definitely at work in this room, Kenan thought. She had lavished great attention and care on the spacious room with its softly colored wall-to-wall carpeting, the lighting designed to enhance the inviting feel.

He felt panicky. "I'd prefer that you accompany me. In case I do have questions," Kenan added quickly. He didn't want her thinking he was a coward, but his voice shook like a house of cards in the wind. "It'll save time if I don't have to go looking for you each time I need information."

Sharley inclined her head slightly. "Certainly."

Her quiet dignity rattled Kenan even more. He wished she would strike up a conversation — about anything. Well, anything but her work. But she seemed to be waiting for him to say something.

Row after row of caskets lined the large showroom, dignified colors with lids open to show the adorned interiors and plush linings. "As you can see, the choice is unlimited." She had shifted into her sales mode. "Maybe you'd like a painted background? Some have verses. A particular color? Wood? This is our most expensive unit in stock."

Kenan wondered about the slight frown that crossed her face. "This particular model is lined with white velvet. The tiny tucks are impressive in themselves."

Kenan moved along the row, finding it difficult to focus. His gaze fixed on the woman's long slender hand as she lovingly stroked the wood, almost as though it was a living thing. For a few moments, he considered how that gentle touch would feel against his skin. Her hand moved to the brass rail that lifted the lid. "This one is solid oak. Impressive, don't you think?"

"Very nice," Kenan said and flinched as he considered what he had just complimented.

Sharley watched Kenan's expression as she lifted the lid slowly. Things shifted into fast and then slow motion. Kenan Montgomery let out an Indian war cry and jumped backward. A serious whack sounded when he struck the casket on the row behind them. A fluorescent yellow smiley face helium balloon floated from the casket and danced along the ceiling.

"Devlin! Jack!" Everyone but the man who lay on the floor could easily hear the shout.

The tall, lanky man ambled into the room, a grin splitting his face. "Yes, ma'am?"

"Is this part of the act?" Sharley asked as she knelt by Kenan's side, noting the pallor of his skin. "He's good," she said. "If I didn't know better, I'd say he's out like a light."

"Act? What are you talking about?"

"This man. The helicopter. That balloon in the casket," Sharley enumerated as she patted the man's hand and cheek. "You guys wasted a lot of money trying to pull one over on me."

A frown creased her employee's face as he knelt by her side. "I don't know who this man is. Jack said we owed you. He knew you'd go in to check the display room, and we figured we could startle you at least."

"Devlin," Sharley said, the growing fear in the pit of her stomach making her nauseous, "please don't tell me this man is a paying customer."

"Sorry, Sharley." His hangdog expression spoke volumes.

"See if there's any ammonia in the first-aid kit." As she spoke, Sharley's hand went to Kenan's wrist. His skin was damp, as though he had been traumatized. Hopefully he hadn't struck his head when he fell. As it was, he would probably sue her into bankruptcy.

Kenan's eyelids fluttered open and shut as the pungent odor tore through his nostrils. He struggled for a few moments, grappling with the hand that seemed so intent on annihilating him. He opened his eyes and looked at the woman who sat back on her heels, obviously dismayed. He remembered where he was and fought his way up. They wouldn't be getting any personal business from him. Not for a long, long time.

"What happened?" A sharp pain shot through his head. Kenan reached to check his skull, wincing when his fingers came into contact with the goose egg.

Her shoulders pushed back, the flaming hair a nimbus around a face that was beautifully serene. Kenan had always thought of undertakers as creepy, but this one was gorgeous. Charlotte Montgomery was almost temptation enough to see if his opinion had been off base all along.

His gaze lingered on the fiery red hair and friendly hazel eyes. Long, the hair draped about her shoulders in curly spirals that made his fingers itch to touch them, to fulfill his overwhelming need to verify that something in this place was full of life. She was nothing like he would have expected to find in a mortician's office. He couldn't stop himself from wondering why she chose to work here when she was definitely suited for more desirable places.

"Do you feel okay? I could run you over to the emergency room if you think you need to be checked out."

He used his long arms to give himself an added boost and got to his feet. "No, I'm fine." Kenan didn't mention the vision that fluttered about in his head. He glanced toward the oak casket and found it to be no more than a long, empty wooden box. His gaze swept along the interior. *Don't be foolish,* he chided his overly active imagination.

Sharley almost screamed when the heat kicked on and the balloon dipped into view. Kenan's face whitened again. So help her, she was going to fire the next employee who pulled a prank. The whole situation was getting out of hand. What had started out as good fun had turned into a nightmare.

"Everything okay, Sharley?"

"It's fine, Devlin. Why don't you get Mr. Montgomery a glass of water?" *And go away,* she cried silently as she noted Kenan's changing expression.

"Mr. Montgomery doesn't want any water, Devlin," Kenan drawled as he grabbed the balloon. "He wants to know why this was inside that casket."

Sharley swallowed and nodded for Devlin to leave her to confront the situation. "I'm sorry. They were playing a joke on me."

His incredulous expression turned the obsidian orbs even blacker. "Joke?" he demanded as he released the balloon and rubbed the bump on the back of his head. "Is that what you call scaring innocent people to death?"

Sharley watched the expressive face change with the mixture of embarrassment and anger. In a flash, she sensed his rage had a much deeper source. This man was no more comfortable now than he had been the moment they met. He was making a poor attempt to cover his fear.

"We're sorry. We never intended to involve anyone else in our little game."

Kenan shrugged this off. "For the life of me, I can't figure out why Samuel Stewart Samuels insists on being buried by you people in this one-horse town anyway."

Sharley's objections were lost at the mention of the man's name. *Samuel Samuels.* Her mother had once joked about parents loving their kids so much they named them twice. It wasn't possible. Was it?

Kenan Montgomery couldn't possibly be talking about the man her mother had jokingly referred to as Triple S. *He doesn't know,* Sharley told herself, fighting the haze that obscured her normal thinking. He couldn't know the man he spoke of was her maternal grandfather, the only living relative she had left in the world, and the man who had walked out on his wife, forgetting the existence of his only daughter.

"Let's just finalize this so I can get out of here," Kenan said, his step quickening as he neared the room's exit. "We'll take the most expensive casket you have."

That was fine with her. Getting him out before he decided to make them pay for his little blackout seemed the best idea she'd heard in a long time.

"Certainly. If you'll step this way, I'll show you the vaults."

A frown cut a groove in the broad forehead. "Don't you have a mausoleum?"

"We don't, but you can always invest in a marble companion mausoleum if you like. Does Mr. Samuels have other family he wants to be interred with?"

"Parents, a wife, and a daughter. They're buried in a family cemetery around here somewhere."

Had her grandfather discussed his family at some point in time with Kenan Montgomery? If so, why didn't he know about her? *Forget it,* Sharley told herself and turned back to the arrangements.

"Do you know if Mr. Samuels has considered cremation?"

"No," Kenan all but shouted. "Sam doesn't want to be burned."

She nodded briefly. "What about body donation?"

He seemed to grow paler with each question she asked. "For heaven's sake, he's seventy-nine years old. I doubt he'd think there was much of his body that's of use to anyone else."

Sharley stepped into the office. "Perhaps you'd like to use the phone to check on his preferences? I could speak to him," she said and then changed her mind. No, she wasn't prepared to speak to her grandfather. Not yet. "Or maybe it would be best if I worked up a proposal. If you'll give me an address, I'd be happy to mail it to you along with literature on the casket and vault for his perusal. I can price the mausoleums if you'd like. Do a couple of scenarios including grave-site burial and a mausoleum."

Her grandmother and mother were buried in the Samuels' family cemetery. Surely her grandfather didn't intend to place himself there as well. They would all turn over in their graves if he did.

Kenan's breathing became shallower with her casual references. He knew that if he didn't get out of there soon, he was going to disgrace himself. How would Charlotte Montgomery react to his throwing up all over her nicely decorated office? He had a feeling she wouldn't appreciate his getting sick on top of her antique desk with its expensive accessories.

"Great idea." He quickly quoted an address. "Mail it to me there and I'll be in touch to finalize the arrangements."

"Is there a number? Just in case I run across something I should call you about."

Kenan watched the red lips speak the words and could think of nothing but removing himself from this nightmare situation. His gaze bolted toward the door. If only he could get his feet into motion.

"Running away won't change anything, Mr. Montgomery."

Her words halted his steps, and his stunned gaze fixed on her knowing expression. She had guessed his secret. Of course, it couldn't have been too difficult for her to pick up on the trail of clues he had left ever since his arrival.

"You're reacting out of fear."

Kenan found her words as chilling as a frigid blast of air-conditioning on a hot summer day. "Just as you're making these plans for someone you love who will one day die, others do the same. Funerals aren't for the deceased. They're for the living. They help people cope with their loss."

His broad chest heaved with the deep breath. He needed air. "Just send the proposal to the address I gave you. We'll be in touch."

Kenan Montgomery charged from her office as if the hounds of hell were nipping at his ankles.

Pity, Sharley thought with a reluctant smile. She could be interested in a man like Kenan Montgomery, and he couldn't get away from her fast enough.

Chapter 2

Kenan glanced about the hotel room, his gaze stopping on the laptop and cellular phone on the dresser. Not even vacation excused failure to contact the office. Sam provided state-of-the-art equipment and demanded that his execs use it at all times. Well, Kenan decided, he'd better check in before taking off for the next leg of his journey.

The phone rang a couple of times before his secretary picked up. "Hi, Marie. How's it going?"

"Kenan, we received an overnight package from Montgomery-Sloan Funeral Home today. It's a quote for funeral arrangements. For Sam."

The hushed fear in his secretary's voice had him rushing to explain. "Which he's not going to need for years. It was something he wanted done. Give me a minute to connect my laptop and fax me a copy."

"Oh." The word sounded more like a relieved sigh. "I'll send it right away."

Charlotte Montgomery must have worked overtime yesterday to assemble all the data she had described. "Give Sam the original packet. Tell him I'll be in touch after I review the information."

"Sure, Kenan. Sam's not . . . He's really okay, isn't he?"

"Sam's getting old. Old people start thinking about death. That's all." Kenan realized her concern was well-placed. Sam Samuels was well-loved by his employees. News of this magnitude in the wrong hands could do worlds of damage. "And Marie, let's keep this low profile. I'm not lying to you, but we don't want this getting out of the office."

The tiny printer produced a facsimile of the correspondence Marie had held in her hands only minutes before. Kenan fingered the letter that accompanied the packet. Charlotte Montgomery must have mailed it just after his departure. He still wasn't certain whether it was eagerness or efficiency.

The proposal workup was uncanny. Not one detail had been missed. That would impress Sam. In fact, it was an aspect Sam demanded in his business ventures. Kenan glanced at the thin gold watch on his wrist and reached for the phone. By now, Sam had reviewed the correspondence. He dialed Sam's private office number.

"Samuels here."

"Hello, Sam."

"Kenan. Glad you called. Enjoying your vacation?"

"Yes, sir. It's been pleasant."

"Good. Good. Just been looking over the information from Montgomery-Sloan."

"What do you think?"

"Very detailed."

"I noted that myself. Marie faxed me a copy." Kenan lifted the letter from the bedspread and glanced over it again. Charlotte Montgomery was obviously no lightweight when it came to business. The stationery lettering was an appropriate Gothic print. The letter had the appearance of being prepared on a computer and printed on a laser printer. The scripture verse caught his eye, Psalm 23:4: "Even though I walk through the valley of the shadow of death, I will fear no evil, for you are with me; your rod and your staff, they comfort me."

"That's weird. Charlotte Claire Samuels Montgomery," Kenan said as he studied the flowing, feminine script of her signature. "I knew about the Montgomery part but not the Samuels. Wonder if that's her maiden name or something?" But she hadn't been wearing a ring. He was sure of it. Kenan always noted details like that.

"What does this woman look like?"

Why would Sam care? Kenan shrugged and described Charlotte in great detail. In the brief time since he'd met Sharley, her beautiful face had imprinted itself on his brain. Once he'd been airborne after escaping her office, he found humor in the incident.

But making a fool of himself in Charlotte Montgomery's eyes annoyed him. It hadn't taken her long to recognize his eagerness to escape. And that one little episode had almost been more than his male ego could bear. Kenan turned beet red at the thought of fainting dead away at her feet. "Why do you ask?"

"I knew someone with that name once," Sam said. Kenan recognized the vagueness as Sam's thinking mode and waited. "Kenan, you've got to go back. I want her in Boston."

He wasn't given to questioning his boss's orders. Usually. But there was something about that place and that woman that got under his skin quicker than chill bumps on a freezing winter day. "Why? You have all the figures, and you have to admit she did an exemplary job." Charlotte Montgomery had covered every possible contingency.

"Very thorough. I want these arrangements finalized, and I want it done in person."

In person with Charlotte Montgomery — *the angel of death,* he thought to himself with a silent groan. In fact, she was quite desirable. Could he put aside his personal feelings of dread long enough to check her out more closely? To see if she was as warm and friendly as she looked?

"Let's just say I have my reasons. Because of that I want you to get to know this Charlotte Samuels Montgomery. I want to know everything you can find out about her."

"I'm not a PI."

"You're the only person I'd trust with this, Kenan."

That was enough for Kenan. Sam had taken him on when he had come home from Vietnam, a broken, confused man, unable to come to grips with what he had witnessed in the foreign jungles. Being placed on a medevac chopper from day one had exposed him to more suffering and loss than he'd ever dreamed possible. It had taken only a few months to come to grips with the fact that he was incapable of dealing with wholesale killing. Fortunately for him, his time had been cut short by the withdrawal of American troops.

Despite their efforts, his family hadn't been able to understand his private torment. His unwillingness to talk only made them more persistent in their efforts to draw him out, and at last he had escaped to Boston and the job with Sam.

When he first put in an application with the company, his experience in flying helicopters appealed to Sam Samuels. In the intervening years, he piloted Sam across the city to and from his country estate. Sam talked, and Kenan listened. Gradually he introduced him to various jobs and Kenan embraced them. He learned more under Sam's tutelage than he could ever have learned in school. Still, Kenan was surprised when the man offered him the position of CEO.

Nothing much had changed. He still flew Sam around the city, but now he handled company business on a daily basis. Sam treated him like a son, and Kenan loved him like a father. So now he did the only thing he could do under the circumstances. "What's the real reason, Sam? We've been together too long for you to start hiding things now."

"I have reason to believe Charlotte Montgomery may be my granddaughter."

Never once had he considered that Charlotte might be related to Sam.

"Her description sounds very much like my late wife," Sam said by way of explanation. "Also Charlotte was my mother's name. I wanted Glory to be named that."

"Glory?"

"My daughter, Gloria. Always hated that name." Sam sounded so distant, as though lost in the past. "I called her Glory."

"What happened? How did you get separated from your family."

"I walked out on them."

"You did what?" Kenan doubted he had heard right. This was God-fearing, good-hearted Sam, not some sorry excuse of a man who would just walk away from his family and not look back.

"I'm not proud of the fact, but I'm not given to making excuses or apologizing either. Jean and I probably should never have married. We were too different. She wanted to live and die in that small town. I wanted to make something of myself."

Kenan was shaken by the truth. "How could you?" he blurted. "How do you justify hurting her like that? And just what do you hope to achieve by making contact with Charlotte Montgomery?"

"Don't judge me, Kenan. God forgave me for my sins. I'm just asking you to help me right a wrong."

"But your daughter . . ."

"Was just a little girl. She had a happier life without me and her mother bickering."

Kenan wondered about his justification. Maybe it made sense, but he felt sorry for the little girl who surely must have felt rejected by her own father. His disappointment at learning his hero had feet of clay weighed heavily on his heart. This certainly wasn't something he had ever thought Sam would do.

At forty-six, Kenan was ready to settle down. The longing for a wife and kids of his own grew stronger by the day. He believed marriage was forever and being a parent was something he could never walk away from. He couldn't understand how Sam could have done so without a backward glance.

"I didn't think it'd be this difficult to convince you," Sam offered.

"I don't want any part of this mess."

"It smacks of hypocrisy, doesn't it?" Sam asked. "I suppose I could order you to do this, but I don't want to. I'm asking you as a friend. There's a lot riding on this. It could be my chance to right a wrong. I didn't do right by my daughter. Perhaps I can do better with my granddaughter."

"I still don't understand how you could do this. It goes against everything I ever believed about you." Kenan's voice was sharp with outrage.

"I'm human, Kenan. Not perfect. I possess all the human frailties others possess, and for a while, I was not walking with our Father. I attribute the entire mess to complete stupidity. It started out with me thinking my wife should believe in me and trust me to do right. Then pride took over, and I decided if my wife didn't want to be with me, I didn't want to be with her. I missed Glory, but I didn't want her caught in the middle. I saw enough of that with my parents. At the time, I thought it my only choice. I can't change things now, I know."

"But you're trying," Kenan conceded. A new thought occurred to him, and he frowned. "What you're doing will affect not only your life but hers as well. Just because you want to relieve your guilt doesn't mean she'll want to cooperate."

Would Sam guess why he was so concerned about Charlotte Montgomery's feelings? Kenan wondered. This went beyond his fear of mortuaries. He found he didn't want Charlotte Montgomery hurt. And if she learned the truth, what an opinion she would have of him. Not only would she think him a coward, she would assume he had been dishonest with her. But if he didn't do what Sam asked, someone else would. Someone who didn't care about anything except the money Sam would pay.

"It's not going to be easy," he said finally, the words followed by a long sigh. "Charlotte Montgomery is an intelligent woman. She'll probably see right through me."

"You're an intelligent man. Healthy, handsome, certainly capable of getting information from this woman."

Kenan knew when he was whipped. "When do you want me to go back?"

"Whenever you're ready. I see no reason for you to interrupt your vacation. The return trip should be time enough."

At almost five in the afternoon, Sharley was ready to hurry home. There was a visitation that night, and she needed to change, eat, and return before the family arrived. As she ran into her office to grab her purse, she was startled to find Kenan Montgomery waiting there.

She had submitted a complete, concise package she felt certain would answer any questions Samuel Stewart Samuels could ask. And though she'd been tempted, she resisted the urge to use the telephone number he'd given her. From Kenan's previous behavior, she was certain nothing short of his own funeral could have convinced him to return to her establishment.

"Mr. Montgomery," she said politely, lifting her hand toward him as she advanced. "I thought you were going to call with your final decision."

"Mr. Samuels preferred I handle the details in person. He was impressed by the proposal you submitted."

"Thank you." *So much for my dinner,* Sharley thought with a sense of disappointment. She had been looking forward to relaxing for a few minutes.

"I know this might sound strange," Kenan said, "but I didn't get lunch today. Do you think we might be able to discuss the arrangements over dinner?"

"I have about forty-five minutes before I need to run home and change for a visitation tonight. There's a barbecue place nearby that has decent food."

"Sounds good. Hope you don't mind driving. I don't think the restaurant would care for my flying us down."

He didn't know much about small towns.

Just seeing the helicopter in the parking lot would give them something to talk about for years. "They'd love it, but I doubt it makes much sense to start it up for a few blocks."

Dinner with Sharley, as she insisted he call her, was interesting. A constant flow of townspeople interrupted their conversation before seating themselves in the restaurant. People spoke to her with smiles and good humor, and she appeared to be well-known, well liked in fact.

Later that evening, Kenan recalled how he had picked up his fork and dug in when their food arrived. He felt like an unmannered oaf when she bowed her head in silent prayer.

He asked a few questions, hoping they didn't sound too contrived, managing to work a few personal points into the conversation, and found she was a woman who laughed often, and usually at herself.

"I owe you an apology. I guess it's more than a little obvious I'm uncomfortable with death."

"You're not alone. Many people are, Kenan. I often seek reassurance from a Higher Power."

"Higher Power?" Kenan frowned. What

was she talking about? "What does that have to do with the way I acted?"

"I find that my belief in God helps me deal with a lot of the life and death issues."

In his own way, Kenan believed in God. As a child, he'd attended church every Sunday with his mother, but the years had separated him from his religion. In Nam, he prayed God would help him through, and He had. The prayers had come less frequently since his return home, though, and his life had moved on.

Kenan squirmed uncomfortably in the chair as Sharley's direct gaze bored into him. "So you're religious?"

"You make it sound like a dreadful disease."

"God doesn't have much use for an old sinner like me."

"We're all sinners, Kenan. Sinners saved by God's grace."

After dinner, they stopped by the chopper to pick up his flight bag, and Sharley dropped him off at the local bed-and-breakfast. Kenan didn't care much for using the phone in the hallway and opted to use his cell phone. It was almost seven. Sam was probably in the office of his palatial estate, going over the myriad details relating to his investments. The man was a workaholic. Perhaps that accounted for the money he'd accumulated in his lifetime. He dialed the private number. Barely half a ring preceded the answer. "Hello, Sam."

"Kenan. Did you see her?"

The eagerness in Sam's voice concerned him. "We had dinner. She's a popular lady. The kids love her. She teaches a Sunday school class of four-year-olds. I think most of them ate in the same restaurant we did tonight."

Sam chuckled. "What do you think?"

Kenan tried to come up with a suitable answer to Sam's question. Some of the thoughts he was having weren't exactly appropriate to share with a grandfather.

"What I think has nothing to do with the situation," Kenan said abruptly.

"Bring her to me."

Sam must think him a miracle worker. Sure, he'd had his share of luck with the opposite sex, but somehow he didn't believe she would agree to the suggestion without question. "Give me one good reason why Charlotte Montgomery would travel to Boston with me?"

"Because you asked her. Nicely, of course."

Kenan chuckled at that. "It might be better if you called and requested a meeting."

"Ask her."

"She might not come."

"Tell her I'm interested in a fifteen- to twenty-thousand-dollar funeral. That should generate enough interest to get her here."

Why not? If she said no, Sam would have to come up with another means of getting her there. "I'll go by the funeral home first thing in the morning."

"I'll see you both in a couple of days."

Kenan sighed as he replaced the phone and reached for his duffel bag. He had no guarantee he would get Sharley to Boston in his lifetime, much less two days. Sometimes Sam placed entirely too much faith in his abilities.

"I'm sorry, sir. Ms. Montgomery won't be in until around eleven."

Kenan frowned. He had wanted to get this over and done with. "I'm really on a tight deadline. Do you have any idea where she might be?"

"Home, I suppose. Though she did mention some errands."

"Is there a cab in this town?"

"Don't need one. Sharley's house is about five blocks from here. Pink Victorian on Montgomery Boulevard. She hates it when we rib her about having her own street.

Only right, though, considering the Montgomerys' contribution to this town. She's got the same blood as two of the town's founding fathers running through her veins."

A warning bell sounded in Kenan's head. The town's founding fathers. Was the Samuels family the other one of those families? "Where is Montgomery Boulevard?" he asked.

Kenan found himself strolling along the quiet streets, wondering how she would respond to his arrival and subsequent inquiry.

The house was just as her employee had described, and Kenan noted her car in the driveway as he rang the bell. When no one answered, he rang it once more. Figuring she was out with someone else, he turned away, stopping when the door opened.

"Kenan? Hello." Sharley pulled the door open wider, her hand going immediately to the barrette that pulled her hair back. She wore a long sweatshirt over a pair of jeans.

"Hope you don't mind. I needed to talk with you."

"Please come in. I was in the attic looking for my grandmother's journals." She indicated the stack of books she held in her other arm. "Samuels is celebrating its bicentennial in October. I'm on the planning committee. We almost have everything pulled together, but I remembered these the other day and thought they might add something to the history."

He nodded and reached to help her with the load. "I called Mr. Samuels last night, and he'd like for you to fly up to Boston with me to discuss your proposal."

"I'm sorry. That's impossible."

If he'd had to describe her changed expression, Kenan would have said Sharley disliked the idea immensely. "If you're worried about time away from the business, we could arrange to have you back within a couple of days." *Sam will kill me for this one,* Kenan thought as he added, "In the event that something should arise, I'm sure Mr. Samuels would be willing to reimburse you for any lost revenue."

They moved into an old-fashioned parlor, furnished with well-maintained antiques that suited the room perfectly. "Have a seat," she invited, indicating the sofa. "I'm afraid I'm a bit confused as to why he would feel it necessary for me to fly to Boston with you."

"Perhaps he was so impressed by your proposal he wants to tell you in person."

Sharley laughed at that. "I'm sure they

have telephones in the big city."

Kenan chuckled. "More than you can count. Seriously, though . . . ," he said, waving one hand through the air. He gasped when he almost toppled the vase that sat on the nearby table. "Whew, that was close."

She moved the urn out of harm's way. *Oh, good,* he thought. Now she'd think he was clumsy, too.

"You'd enjoy the trip," he said, jumping immediately into his travel plans. "I could call for the company jet to meet us at the airport. I'd need to put the chopper in storage there. Have you ever flown in one?" At her negative head movement, he continued, "You'd like the chopper. There's nothing like it. Up there, just above land, close enough to see everything, your body vibrating with the machine."

"Sounds intriguing." She appeared thoughtful, her gaze moving to the vase and back to him.

"Will you go?"

She nodded. "On one condition."

"What's that?" he asked curiously.

"We scatter the contents of that urn."

Kenan glanced at the vase, and understanding knotted his stomach. "Who is it?"

"My father. He always wanted to go skydiving but decided it wasn't something a mortician would do," Sharley explained. "This would be the closest I'm ever likely to get. I'm not even the mental daredevil my father was. I don't fantasize about jumping out of a plane, and it's highly unlikely I could manage the vase and a parachute even if I did."

Kenan felt the color drain from his face.

"Of course I'd understand if you'd rather not," she tacked on hurriedly.

He wouldn't let Sam down. "When can you leave?"

"Not until tomorrow. We have a funeral this afternoon at three. And I'll need to make sure everything is covered here. Say eight in the morning."

"I'll be waiting. I have reservations at the bed-and-breakfast again tonight."

"I could pick you up if you'd like. I'll leave my car at the office."

"If it's not too much bother."

"Not at all," Sharley said with a broad smile. "After all, we'll be taking your vehicle to the airport."

Sharley spent the hours after the funeral making arrangements to have the office covered during her absence. Jack Jennings and Devlin Spear were her right hands. Though neither of them liked being in charge, they were more than capable.

Jack was as much a part of Montgomery-Sloan as the building. He was a distant cousin her dad hired when he took over the business. Sharley couldn't remember a time when he hadn't been around. Jack was in his fifties when she took over management. Sharley feared he would resent her or quit even, but he had turned out to be a valued employee and friend.

Devlin Spear was a more recent addition. In his early twenties, his friendly nature had impressed Sharley from their first meeting. Devlin was a good addition to their crazy crew. She felt comfortable knowing they were taking care of Montgomery-Sloan.

Her thoughts drifted back to Kenan Montgomery. Did he really think she had no idea who Samuel Samuels was? It might not have been a popular name in her house during her childhood, but it had been mentioned more than a time or two. Maybe she should just tell him she knew.

She grinned. On second thought, she wouldn't tell him anything. She wanted to carry out her father's last wish, and she doubted Kenan would be half as agreeable if he knew the truth.

She owed this to her father. Jackson

Montgomery had let propriety keep him from enjoying life. Dealing with that same propriety was Sharley's greatest struggle. She expressed her opinion and dealt with the many qualities that kept her from being the proper mortician, but thanks to God's help, she managed to keep things under control enough to project a suitable image. Still, she rebelled from time to time. And then she prayed even harder for the Lord's help.

On his deathbed, her father had told her he should have done a few of those things he'd wanted to do. He encouraged her to try things before it was too late. That was when Sharley had promised herself to make sure his ashes were scattered from the sky. In the intervening months, she had been unable to work up the nerve to do it herself. She had considered hiring someone, but she knew the likelihood of finding a willing person would be less if they knew what she had in mind.

This would be perfect. Obviously Samuel Samuels wanted her in Boston badly enough that Kenan Montgomery was willing to go along with her request. Her father's last wish would be carried out, and she had found a means that didn't entail her jumping from a plane — and for that she would do anything, including meet her grandfather.

Sharley whispered a prayer for strength. Sometimes being a Christian was hard work. She didn't want to hold a grudge against Sam Samuels. She wanted to forgive and forget and maybe even get to know the man her mother had never known.

"Please, God. You know how hard this is for me."

Kenan had been right about one thing. Sharley loved the helicopter. She climbed into the front passenger seat and strapped herself in, accepting the headset he handed her. *It's like riding in a glass bubble,* she thought as she looked through the window at her feet. The steady whirring of the blades vibrated the chopper. Kenan set the chopper into motion, and they twirled in a circle, tilting to one side as they moved higher.

The view below held Sharley fascinated. The area was alive with the new growth of spring, lush greenery covering the formerly bare trees. Patches of color here and there indicated the spring flowers.

Every once in a while someone came along selling aerial photos of the houses in town, and most people purchased one of their home. Still the black-and-white shots did nothing to depict the true vision Mother Nature had bequeathed on Samuels.

"Look down." Kenan's voice filled her ears, and Sharley jumped. "See it?"

She grinned at him. "It's my house. And there's the funeral home." Sharley continued to point out various sites.

Soon, Samuels was behind them and she was initiated to more beauty. Furrowed rows in fields that had lain barren over winter months. Tractors moving slowly back and forth as farmers planted their crops.

"Is this what you had in mind?" Kenan asked as they flew past a group of trees.

Sharley looked down. Exactly the place she loved to roam through at her leisure. She nodded. They hovered as Kenan told her how to open the window. Wind gusted into the chopper, and the lid fell off the vase when she pulled back.

"Be careful with that thing," Kenan shouted over the noise of the blades. "I don't want your father's ashes in my face."

Sharley smiled. Kenan Montgomery didn't want anything near him that had to do with death. The psychologist in her made Sharley want to broach the topic, but she didn't think he would be very receptive to the discussion.

In seconds the deed was done. Her father's

ashes blew over the field, the downdraft from the chopper blades helping to scatter them.

"Thank you," Sharley whispered as she refitted the headset into place.

Kenan's eyes held hers with a strange intensity. "You okay?"

She nodded, a glimmer of tears in her hazel eyes. When he reached out to her, Sharley offered her hand in return. In that brief touch, they shared something extremely important. Kenan cared. He didn't say the words. There was no need. Gladness and warmth filled her heart.

"It's going to be all right," he said, flashing her a reassuring smile as he set the chopper back on course.

Chapter 3

Sharley's first face-to-face look at the man who was her grandfather took her by surprise. He appeared younger than his almost eighty years. So much so that she found it difficult to imagine he was even thinking about his funeral. He looked to be in excellent health.

He stood and extended his hand. "Ms. Montgomery, thank you for coming."

"My pleasure, Mr. Samuels."

"Call me Sam."

Sharley tilted her head to one side, appearing puzzled as she asked, "Does one call their grandfather by his first name?"

"You knew?" Kenan's words sounded more like an accusation.

"Of course I did," she returned, her hazel eyes pinpointing him in a direct stare. "Even though we've never met before, my parents did acquaint me with my grandfather's name. I've even seen an old photograph or two."

"I'll be in my office if you need me."

Sharley looked at Sam as Kenan stormed from the room. "I think he's angry."

"He'll get over it."

"I should have told him," she said, shrugging at her run-in with good intentions. "I had always assumed you died years ago. My father only told me you were still alive shortly before his own death."

"I suppose you expect an apology for what I did to Jean and Glory?"

Sharley considered his statement, particularly his name for her mother. She liked it; Glory suited her more than Gloria ever had. Sharley herself rarely apologized for her own actions. Maybe it was a part of her genes she had inherited from the Samuels side. "No."

"Then maybe you realize I've got some money? Are you expecting your share?"

Sharley grinned. She had money, too. Her father's family hadn't been as wealthy as her grandfather, but he'd left her well provided for. Besides, her business fell into one of the earning categories. Along with taxes and birth, death was one of life's certainties, a recession-proof career. "Congratulations, but no again."

"Then what do you expect from me?"

"Absolutely nothing. You're hardly an old man with a deathbed plea for forgiveness. And I'm not a destitute young woman seeking reconciliation with her grandfather. I'm here for the same reason you wanted me here — curiosity. I'd like to know a little about the Samuels blood that runs through my veins. This is my chance to find out."

"So you don't doubt we're related?"

Sharley shook her head. "I knew the day Kenan told me your name. I've heard it often enough. Samuel Stewart Samuels. My mom called you Triple S."

The gray eyebrows were a sharp contrast to the snow-white hair as they jutted upwards. "Not always in the best of terms, I imagine."

"Actually neither Mommy Jean nor Mother ever said anything derogatory. Besides, I could hardly call myself a Christian if I sat in judgment of you. Grandmother and Mother made their peace with the situation."

The familiar smile showed itself on Sam's face. "You can't know how thrilled I am to hear you know the Lord."

Sharley smiled back at him. "I'm thrilled to have Him in my life."

Sam nodded, and Sharley knew he understood the feelings she tried to communicate in her witness to nonbelievers. "Praise the Lord, our God is a forgiving God," he said. "Have dinner with me at my house tonight? I could ask Kenan to join us if you like."

She considered it. She liked the idea a lot, but she didn't think Kenan would be interested. He'd been in a fine rage when he stormed out of the office. Probably more than a little ticked off at her for the condition she had set when all along she would have come anyway. "After what I put him through on the trip up, I'd think he'd rather not."

Sharley launched into a description of their two meetings that had Sam chuckling. "I don't think he's comfortable around death," she concluded.

"Few people are. Kenan has more reason not to be than others. He flew a medevac chopper in Nam for a while."

Maybe that was it, but Sharley sensed his fears ran deeper.

"What about dinner? Maybe I am an old man interested in making things right before I go. I'd really like it if you would stay at my house while you're in town."

She considered his offer. At this stage of the game it would be ridiculous for her to climb on her high horse to defend her mother's honor. Gloria Samuels Montgomery had been more than capable of fighting her own battles. If there had been something she wanted to say to her father, she would have done so in no uncertain terms. In death, as in life, she didn't need a protector. "It would be my pleasure."

He smiled, and Sharley found something else she had inherited from Sam Samuels. She flashed him a matching wide and friendly smile.

"Now about these proposals you sent me," Sam said, indicating the papers spread about his desktop. "Do I get a family discount?"

"Why should I?" Sharley countered. "A girl has to make a living, you know."

Kenan suggested she make herself comfortable for the drive out to Sam's country estate in Dover.

"We don't have to go through that tunnel again, do we?"

Sharley had been glad of the limo's dark windows when Kenan indicated they were traveling underwater.

"What? Does Sharley Montgomery have a phobia?"

"I don't swim."

Kenan laughed at that. "And I left all the

life jackets at the office."

Sharley focused her attention on the passing scenery, and after a while, he asked, "Why didn't you tell me you knew?"

She looked at Kenan. "Why didn't you tell me?"

"It wasn't my place."

"I'm not going to argue the point with you, Kenan. I could have kept pretending not to know and let the truth come out later, but it wouldn't have served any true purpose. Sam's been out of my life forever. At least I'm trying to be civilized about the matter. He asked me to stay at his house, and I will. I'm not after his money or trying to hurt him. I just wanted to meet my sole surviving relative and maybe get to know him. And yes, I probably owe you an apology for that trick with Daddy's ashes, but I don't think you would have been as receptive to the idea if you hadn't wanted something, too."

A frown touched his handsome face. "To tell you the truth, I don't particularly care for the way either of you has used me."

"You think Sam knew I existed when he sent you to Samuels?"

At his hesitation, Sharley knew Kenan was giving the matter serious consideration. "Probably. When he saw the way you signed your proposal, he asked what you looked like and insisted on seeing you."

"It was his mother's name."

Charlotte found herself lost deep in thought, going back through the years to the time when a ten-year-old asked her mother why her grandmother always seemed so upset when her grandfather's name was mentioned.

Gloria Samuels Montgomery had hugged Sharley close. "The past wasn't kind to your grandmother, darling. She loved my father, and he went away. She sometimes blames herself for his leaving."

"Because she didn't name you Charlotte?"

Her mother had soothed a hand over her black hair. "Oh, Sharley, sometimes you're much too wise for your years. My father begged her to name me Charlotte after his mother, and she wouldn't. But no, it wouldn't have changed anything."

"Because she didn't like the name?"

"No, darling, it's a beautiful name. I'm glad your father wanted me to name you after your great-grandmother and my family. I only wish we had been able to give you a brother or sister to play with."

"Oh, Mama," she had cried when the tears trailed along her mother's cheeks, "I like being your only baby."

"And I couldn't have had a better one if I'd gone to heaven and personally picked you out," she always declared, brushing her lips against Sharley's cheek.

These special times with her mother had been the moments Sharley missed so deeply since her passing. It seemed more like forever than only a couple of brief years; time had a way of healing, though, and she was going on.

She liked to believe that her mother had been proud that she had followed in her father's footsteps. Gloria Samuels Montgomery had been proud of her husband. She had teased him out of his sometimes withdrawn stance and put a smile on his face that had changed him into a likable fellow.

Her mother had often claimed responsibility for changing his image with the public. Her eyes would twinkle as she teased him mercilessly about how he had frightened kids as a scowling old undertaker until she had turned him around.

Sharley had laughed with her father. As she had grown older and begun to understand the love her parents shared, she hoped that one day she would find a man she could tease and love as much as her mother had loved her father. She was still looking, though, sometimes wondering if there was a man who was capable of dealing with all the complexities that made up Charlotte Montgomery.

"Sharley?" Kenan's hand on her arm brought her back to reality. She reached up to dash away the tears that trembled on long lashes, covering her emotions with a trembly smile.

"I'm sorry, too," he said. "I shouldn't have taken part in the ruse to get you here. But he was determined. I didn't know who he would involve if I didn't help him. It's just that . . . Well, Sam . . . he's a wealthy man. . . ."

"And as peculiar as they come," Sharley offered, her face stretching in a wide grin. "I'm not exactly average either. Maybe that's another of those things I inherited from the Samuels side."

The conversation drifted to safer subjects as Kenan told Sharley about the area.

"I can't believe you've never been to Boston."

"I never traveled much. I even went to college in North Carolina. Mommy Jean took me to New York on a culture trip when I was about eight. I cried and told her I wanted to go home. I must have been really bad. She cut the trip short."

"I bet you were a character even then."

Sharley laughed and said, "I am what I am. No sense in pretending any different."

"We're here."

The mansion sat directly in front of where he had stopped his Mercedes in the driveway. Sharley let out an impressed whistle. "This is some house."

"Sam likes his space."

"I don't think we can find anything this big to put him away in."

"Please," Kenan said, shuddering with distaste. "Let's don't even discuss that. Sam asked me to bring you home and get you settled. He'll be home by seven. Dinner is served at seven fifteen."

"Are you coming?"

His eyes focused on her, and Sharley felt a growing warmth at the appreciation she saw in their depths. "He invited me."

She grabbed his arm. "Please. I think maybe you might serve as a buffer between us."

"Why would you need a buffer?"

"Because I suspect we're more alike than is good for either of us," she responded with a cheeky grin. "You already know we both like our way too much for our own good."

Kenan chuckled. "I do. The similarities between the two of you are incredible.

What's strange is that I didn't even see them until you were both in the same room. I was floored earlier by how alike you are when you smile. I think maybe you've got him slightly off balance, too."

"So you'll come?"

"Sure. If you promise not to talk about your job."

"Why does it bother you, Kenan?"

His expression closed. "It just does. Let's get you settled in. I'm supposed to sit in on a meeting with Sam this afternoon."

He'd tell her one day, Sharley vowed. "Really? What exactly do you do for Sam?"

"My official title is chief executive officer but it should be gofer."

The car filled with the sound of her laughter. "Somehow I don't think that would impress the people with the big bucks no matter how appropriate it might be."

At dinner that night Sharley mentally prayed her thanks for living in a small country town. Sam's house was huge. Just leaving her bedroom was an adventure. She'd gotten lost twice trying to find the dining room. His table seemed a mile long, him seated at one end, her at the other. Kenan sat halfway down.

She responded to Sam's questions, repeating her answers when he couldn't hear what was said. This was ridiculous. Her table for six was far more desirable than this.

"Charlotte? Where are you going?" Sam demanded when she stood and grabbed up her plate and utensils.

"You staying down here in the echo chamber or moving up in the world?" she asked as she passed Kenan's chair.

He grinned and quickly gathered his place setting to follow.

Sharley sat down to her grandfather's right, leaving the opposite side for Kenan. "I refuse to raise my voice unless we're having a shouting match. This room is too big and too cold."

"Not when it's filled with guests," Kenan volunteered.

"Is that often?" Sharley countered.

"Fairly. Sam likes to entertain."

"Surely there's a smaller table in this house."

"The breakfast room seats twelve," Sam volunteered.

"Twelve?" Sharley repeated. "You don't do anything in half measures, do you?"

"There's a table for four in the kitchen," Kenan said.

Sharley could tell by Kenan's smile that the picture of his employer seated in the kitchen nudged his funny bone. "There's nothing wrong with that," Sharley said when his laughter broke free. "I often sat at the kitchen table while my mother was cooking and talked with her."

"Your mother cooked?" Kenan asked.

"My mother did a lot of things. Samuels isn't exactly a bustling metropolis, and while I may live in a nice home on a street named after my ancestors, my neighbors don't expect me to get above my raising."

"Jean was a marvelous cook," Sam reminisced. "What that woman could do with chocolate layer cake was beyond words."

"Mother improved on her recipe," Sharley said with a smile. "Daddy used to declare he was glory-bound when he took a bite."

Sam appeared thoughtful for a few minutes before he blurted out, "I hope Glory forgave me."

"She once told me you wanted a life without her. She learned to live that way. There were three times when I think she might have considered looking for you, but she never did."

"When?"

"When she married Daddy, when I was born, and when Mommy Jean was diagnosed with cancer."

Sam cleared his throat. "What did she do

with her life?"

"Became the first lady of Samuels."

"First lady?"

Sharley grinned. "She got Daddy elected mayor. You should have seen him. He blustered and said he didn't want it. Told her to run herself. She told him she didn't want to be mayor, just first lady. And she was a lady. He was putty in her hands." Sharley's eyes teared with the thought. Her mother had been a regal and beautiful role model. "She also worked in the business and dedicated her life to showing people our human side."

"What did she tell you about me?"

Sharley laid down her fork and looked Sam directly in the eye. "That's the second time you've asked how Mother felt about you. What do you want me to tell you? That she hated you and would never have approved of my coming here? That she and Grandmother had to fight to get beyond the fact that the descendant of the town's founding father deserted the town?"

His expression told Sharley nothing, and suddenly she felt ashamed of the way she had allowed her temper to take control.

"She didn't, you know," she said softly. "Neither Mother nor Grandmother ever spoke a word against you. They believed in people being happy. Both of them hoped you were."

"I can't say whether you're your mother's daughter, but I can see Jean in you," Sam said. "Maybe I'm feeling remorse in my old age. Not that I'd change things. I wouldn't go back to Samuels, but maybe I would have tried harder to convince my family to come with me." Sam pushed his plate away. "I remember your grandfather Montgomery. Smoked a cigar with him when your father was born. Cecil Montgomery was a boring man."

"Yes, he was," Sharley agreed. "Mother once said it was a good thing most of the people he dealt with were already dead."

Sharley saw Kenan shake his head at her funeral home humor.

"I bet Cecil never walked away from the honor of being a founding father," Sam said.

"Daddy always said Grandfather considered it good for business. Mother said he was so delighted when she agreed to marry Daddy that he insisted Mommy Jean allow him to help with the wedding plans. It was quite some affair. I have the picture album and copies of the papers with the write-ups of the wedding at home. Mother made certain Daddy didn't follow in his footsteps. She kept him from getting stuffy. She loved Daddy. And she loved Samuels."

"And you? Is that small town enough for you?"

"My life is full. Work and church keep it that way."

"What about marriage?" Kenan asked. "You can't take a career and religion home with you at night."

"I'd disagree with you on that. My work is fulfilling, and my relationship with God gives meaning to my entire life. Mother and I were really close, and I'm very like her in the respect that I love Samuels. I love being a descendant of the town's founding fathers. And I have political aspirations of my own. I have no intention of merely being the supporting woman behind the candidate, though."

Out of deference to Kenan's request that she not talk about her job, Sharley didn't mention the elected position she planned to pursue. She also left it unsaid that her mother had always wanted a warm, loving relationship with her family. She knew now was not the time for recriminations, and her place wasn't to criticize her grandfather for what he had done to her mother.

Gloria Montgomery had once told Sharley she wasn't sure she ever wanted to see her father again. Her feelings for him had been more like those for a parent who had died during her childhood. She had said she couldn't even recall his face without the aid of her mother's pictures. Maybe that was where she had learned not to cry for what she couldn't have.

Her grandfather asked more questions about Sharley's mother, and she answered as best she could. "She was very popular in high school. A cheerleader and valedictorian of her class."

"I always knew Glory was smart, Charlotte."

"Very. I have a nickname, too, you know."

He nodded. "Just where did *Sharley* come from?"

She lifted her shoulders. "The Montgomery penchant for nicknames, I guess. Daddy called me his Charlie girl a time or two when I was three or four, and I told him I weren't no boy; so he started calling me his Sharley girl, and it stuck."

Sam nodded again. "Tell me more."

"I took after Mother. I was valedictorian, too, and graduated magna cum laude from college. I majored in psychology and minored in business management. I also have a mortuary science degree."

Sharley launched into the story of her parents' romance. "Mother and Daddy met right after she came home from college.

When a great-aunt died, Mother attended her visitation, and that was when she met Daddy. He was training to take over for his father. She told me once that she was afraid to approach him at first. But attraction was stronger, and she made excuses to see Jackson Montgomery. Mommy Jean told her she was foolish to fall in love with an undertaker."

"Jean would feel that way," her grandfather agreed with a wry grin.

"Mom told her true love was never foolish. She and Dad had almost forty happy years together. She died in her sleep a couple of years ago."

"And your dad?"

"He died last year."

"So you've run the business alone for the past year?"

"Actually I've been in charge for longer than that. Daddy had emphysema. He was on oxygen for a couple of years before he died. He felt it was okay for him to work in the back, but mine was the public face. He listened to my presentations over the intercom and advised me on changes to make in the future. I learned a lot from him when it came to the business end of things."

"Have you considered leaving the business for something else? You could write your own ticket at Samuels Enterprises."

"Based on an acquaintance of a couple of hours?" Sharley said, disbelief coloring her words. "I'm truly honored, but no thanks. I don't want to make changes in my life."

"Are you trying to shock an old man by admitting that a beautiful woman like you prefers the funeral home business?"

"No. I don't mind admitting I love my line of work. I had a lot of options open to me, but I knew it was what I wanted to do. The psychology degree was so I could help the bereaved. A Montgomery has operated the funeral home in Samuels for almost two hundred years. I just hope my kids want to carry on the tradition."

"Speaking of kids, just when do you plan to have them? You're what? Twenty-five?" Sam guessed.

"Didn't anyone ever tell you about asking a woman's age?" she teased. Sharley didn't mind telling anyone how old she was. She wore every one of her years with as much grace as possible.

"Hey, I'll be eighty soon, and I'm proud of it. Besides, I'm not asking any woman. I'm asking my granddaughter."

"I'm thirty-five," Sharley told him. "We share more than a name, actually. I was born on your birthday."

She could tell he was pleased, but he merely said, "The biological clock's been ticking away for a few years, hasn't it?"

Sharley grinned at his less-than-tactful reference to her advanced years. She wanted a family more than anything else in the world, but she had yet to meet the man she wanted to father her children. "There's more to bringing a child into the world than just biology," she said softly. "I want my children to feel loved and wanted; I want them to grow up knowing God. In fact, I believe God wants me to wait for the man He created to help me raise my children in just that way. Hopefully he'll come along soon. Meanwhile, I have an entire group of children at church. A Sunday school class of preschoolers."

"But they aren't yours."

"Nope, but they're good experience for when I have my own. I love working with them."

Sam was silent for a moment. "What about you, Charlotte?" he asked at last. "How do you feel about what I did to your mother?"

Sharley fiddled with her napkin, pleating and then smoothing the creases from the fabric before she balled it up and placed it on the table by her plate. "I'm going to say this, and then I'm going to extract a promise from you, Papa Sam. I think that you cheated a lot of people with your actions. You deprived Mommy Jean of a husband, Mother of a father, me of a grandfather, and the people of Samuels of a leader and friend. You've accomplished a lot here in Boston, but I think maybe you could have done the same for Samuels.

"But it wasn't my choice to make, nor is it my role in life to judge. I can't promise you that I'm not going to remind you of Mother or some way she might have suffered because you weren't there — but I'm going to try not to. For you and me, life started today. So if you're willing to accept me as I am, I promise to do the same for you."

His hand covered hers, and she squeezed it, noting the misty sheen of his eyes. "It's a deal, Charlotte."

"I'd really like it if you called me Sharley."

They smiled at each other. "You know, I sort of like this new seating arrangement," Sam announced. "Kenan, remind me to tell Elise to group small parties like this from now on."

"Yes, sir," Kenan said.

"Why don't you take Sharley out and show her what I pay those gardeners a small fortune for?"

"Sharley?"

She stood, not too sure what they would see in the darkness. "I'd love to see the gardens. I caught a glimpse from my balcony earlier."

Side by side, they strolled along lighted pathways that were intricately worked between flowers and plants too numerous to count.

"It's beautiful," Sharley murmured as she stopped to smell a rose that had wrapped itself around the archway separating the rose garden from the other areas. "Makes my gardening efforts look shabby."

"It suits the house," Kenan said. "You suit this place."

Sharley waved her hands airily. "Do you mean I have a lady-of-the-manor look?"

Kenan pulled her into his arms, and their lips met in a soft, stirring kiss.

Sharley felt dazed by the impact as he released her, and they took a couple of steps apart. Her hand went to her mouth.

"Sorry," Kenan said, a strange catch in his voice. "I didn't mean to spring it on you like that."

"But you intended to kiss me? You were just going to warn me ahead of time?"

"I — I think so."

A giggle rose up into her throat, and Sharley forced it back as she considered his response. "So give me that warning next time. Okay?"

"Okay."

It was over and done with, and yet she knew the kiss had made a difference. Sharley felt slightly unsettled by the charge that shot through her when Kenan took her hand and pulled her arm through his. As they strolled, she realized he wasn't going to be just another man.

"Well, what do you think?" she asked in an effort to regain control. "Will Sam and I be able to keep the agreement?"

"I suppose you will if you both work at it."

"Probably so. When we're together, that is. Our lives are so far removed from each other."

"What do you mean?"

"Just that Triple S isn't moving to Samuels, and I'm not moving here. We should be capable of being cordial to each other on the rare occasions when we find ourselves in each other's company."

"But surely . . . I mean, now that you know you have a grandfather . . . and that's no way to refer to your grandfather."

"You think I'd give up my life in favor of

developing a closer relationship with him?"

"Well . . . yes, I do. It's not every day you learn you have a grandfather."

"Kenan, I knew I had a grandfather when I was a small child. That didn't keep me from living my life up to this point. Nor did it keep Sam from doing the same. I don't think he expects anything to change, and neither do I."

"It's wrong. Both of you are throwing away something very precious here."

"No, Kenan. We've found something precious, and if it's precious enough, we'll both work to overcome the problems."

"Maybe you're right."

"I know I am." She hesitated and then added, "I've been thinking about what you said earlier, and I've decided you were right. I did use you today, and I'm sorry. Maybe if I had asked, you would have said no to my request for help with Daddy's ashes — but you would have been entitled."

Kenan was silent for several seconds before he trailed a finger along her cheek. "I wouldn't have said no. I could see it was important to you."

Sharley smiled. "Does that mean you never say no?"

"Sometimes I have to. When I was in Nam, I learned life was a big maybe. I guess maybe that still tempers a lot of my decisions."

"Sam was lucky to have found you," she whispered.

"I was the lucky one. We'd better go back. Sam's probably waiting for his coffee."

Kenan led the way to the room Sharley figured was probably Sam's home office and library. It was her favorite of the rooms she'd seen thus far. Book-lined walls, a massive fireplace with a fire in the grate, and sturdy, comfortable masculine furniture.

Sam asked Sharley to pour for them, and they settled in with their coffee and dessert.

"I need to be getting home," Kenan announced, placing his empty cup and saucer on the tray.

"You could stay over tonight and drive in with me tomorrow," Sam suggested.

"I have those files for our meeting to go over again."

"Don't understand why we can't reschedule."

"Why would you want to? It took two months to set it up."

"I'd like to spend time with my granddaughter."

"Then let's get things wrapped up as quickly as possible tomorrow."

Sharley's gaze shifted from Kenan to Sam.

Was he considering canceling the meeting that had taken so long to set up? Surely not. "I'll be here when you get home," she told Sam. "Don't forget, you're dealing with a businesswoman here. I know all about these important meetings."

"I'll see myself out then," Kenan said. "Good night, Sharley."

"Thank you again for everything," she said softly.

Kenan's gaze caught hers and held. "It's been my pleasure. Let me know if there's anything I can do."

"I will."

"Wait, Kenan. Let me get that other file for you."

Both men walked over to the desk and were soon involved in the papers Sam produced.

Sharley's thoughts kept going back to Kenan's surprise kiss. He was about as subtle as a teenage boy on his first date. *Should I?* she imagined him thinking. *Shouldn't I? Oh, go ahead and get it over with already.* This time her giggle erupted, and she covered her face, certain Kenan wouldn't care for her analogy of their romantic interlude. If that was what you called it.

She looked up and caught Kenan and

Sam staring at her. Though she felt a little foolish, Sharley flashed them a brilliant smile. Kenan called good night and walked out of the room. After he left, Sam concentrated the conversation back on her. "Thank you for agreeing to stay with me," Sam said. "I hope your room is okay?"

"It's beautiful. Your home is magnificent."

"I've instructed the housekeeper to serve you breakfast in bed. There's an intercom near the nightstand. Just let her know when you're ready."

"That's not necessary. I can get up and eat with you."

Sam frowned even more heavily than he had when Kenan had reminded him of the meeting earlier. "Unfortunately, I have appointments scheduled for all day tomorrow. I hoped to get out of them, but Kenan assures me it's impossible."

"There's no reason why you should. It's business. I can certainly understand that."

"I don't like inviting you to stay with me and then leaving you to entertain yourself. I can't even ask Kenan to fill in for me because he's involved in these pesky meetings as well."

"It's no problem. Really."

"Perhaps you'd like to do some sightseeing. I can make the limo and driver available to you. You could go shopping."

"I think I'll stay put and enjoy my surroundings. For some reason, I just feel like being lazy."

"Do you swim? There's a heated pool — or a spa, if you prefer. If you'll tell me your size, I'll have Elise send for swimsuits."

Pools. Spas. Swimsuits just by mentioning my size. What luxury. Sharley smiled. "That's not necessary. Don't worry about me. I'll spend at least half the day finding my way around. In fact, I'll probably just be getting downstairs by the time you arrive home from work."

Sam laughed. "Perhaps I should ask Elise to provide a tour guide."

"That sounds like something I really could use. Now, tell me why you never contacted Mother," Sharley asked, making herself more comfortable by shifting her legs underneath her and leaning into the corner of the comfortable sofa.

"Glory visited me once."

Sharley sat up straight. "When? I thought you said you never heard from Mother."

Sam offered her a mint from the dish on the table and then took one for himself. He slipped it into his mouth. "She was eighteen, fresh out of high school and full of herself," he reminisced. "A beauty. She asked me to come back to Samuels. I told her I couldn't and never saw or heard from her again."

"Why couldn't you go back?"

"I had to be in a place where I could be me, Sharley. Not Stewart Samuels's hard-headed son. At least that's what I thought at the time."

"But what about Jean Samuels's husband and Gloria Samuels's father? Weren't those roles important to you?"

"We could go round and round on stupidity and pride, but we wouldn't accomplish any more than your mother and I did. The ties in Samuels strangled me."

"We're different in that respect."

"You got that from Jean. Sometimes I felt she loved my place in the community more than me. She changed even more when Glory was on the way. Started siding with my father. Saying things would be easier if I'd try harder. I tried. I really did, but I'm not a conformist. Never have been."

"Neither am I," Sharley argued.

"But you found a way to belong. I never did."

"Maybe it's different for me because I'm the only Samuels in town. There's no one for people to compare me to."

"I can't say why one person loves a place while another hates it passionately. I hated

Samuels. I don't regret leaving. I do regret losing Jean and Glory and even you." He looked thoughtful. "My search for happiness ended the day I got back in the right relationship with God. Unfortunately it was too late by then to make things right with Jean and Glory."

"Did you know about me?"

"I knew Glory had married and had a child. But on the day she stormed out of here, she demanded that I stay out of her life. I honored her wishes. I didn't go to Jean's funeral because of Glory. I couldn't hurt her anymore."

"I understand."

He flashed her a grin. "Then maybe you'd care to explain it to me."

Sharley laughed and shook her head. "Papa Sam, you're one in a million."

"So are you, Sharley girl. So are you."

Kenan Montgomery unlocked the door of his Mercedes and climbed inside. The engine remained silent as he sat there in Sam's driveway, his thoughts filled with the woman he had discovered tonight.

To say Charlotte Samuels Montgomery intrigued him would be the biggest understatement in the world. He was intrigued, bedazzled, and amazed. There he went again, his mind listing words quicker than he could blink his eyes. If nothing else, she was Sam's female equivalent. They were so alike it was shocking. He could have raised her.

Except for one thing: Kenan couldn't understand her love of small towns. Like Sam, he loved the bustle of the big city. He liked having things to do and places to go. What was there to do in a small town?

His thoughts took a different direction. With a woman like Sharley, a man could while away the hours without realizing they had passed. He had watched her hair ripple and flash in the candlelight as she talked. She had worn a simple dress that proved she liked the world knowing she was a woman, but she didn't feel the need to be overly informative in the fact.

And a psychologist. That news had floored him. What on earth would have made her pursue such a degree if she intended to run a funeral home? No wonder she had asked why death bothered him. His reaction probably intrigued her.

Maybe he should have told her. Kenan longed to shed the lifetime of fears that had bedeviled him, but he knew he didn't know Charlotte Montgomery well enough to unburden himself.

Not that he wouldn't like to know her better. But she was Sam's granddaughter. He owed the man too much to chase after his only living relative unless his intentions were honorable. In his heart Kenan knew they could never be. He was too locked up inside himself to ever be a good husband to a woman who was a mortician. And he sure didn't plan on fathering a bunch of little kids to push into the funeral business.

Chapter 4

"I'll expect to hear from you by Monday." Sharley replaced the receiver and let out a long sigh. She had just spent over an hour trying to straighten out a burial policy and knew even less now than before.

One of those days — scratch that, one of those weeks with snafu after snafu. At least it was Friday afternoon, and her weekend appeared to be free. Sharley lifted the folder and came across the information on replacing the hearse and limos. It wasn't going to be cheap.

Ideally she would have ordered three vehicles in either pearl gray or white, whichever of the two colors she considered classier at the time. But as a businesswoman on her own, working hard to keep her profits on an even keel, Sharley worried about the sizable investments.

Of course, at this rate it wouldn't make much difference anyway. There weren't any little Montgomerys to take her place. There wouldn't be any little Montgomerys anyway. Unless her husband took her name or she married someone named Montgomery. Someone like Kenan Montgomery.

Sure, like there was a chance of that happening. *Stop feeling sorry for yourself,* Sharley chided herself as a wave of dissatisfaction flooded through her. She had felt this way ever since Kenan had brought her home. Things had settled back to normal and though the Denton funeral went off beautifully, her former spirits were still not restored.

She couldn't erase Kenan from her thoughts. His strong reaction to death worried her, along with his closeness to Sam. Both were solid reasons for her not to become involved with him. But though she didn't want to be, she was attracted to him.

On one hand, a man who disliked anything to do with death as much as Kenan did surely couldn't accept a woman who made her living from it. And on the other hand, how could she be sure he was interested in her for herself and not for her wealthy grandfather?

She shook her head. Where had that come from? Kenan wasn't interested in her at all. The idea was so off base it was laughable.

When he'd brought her home, he had all but thrown her out of the chopper before the rotors stopped turning. She had offered him a room, so he could get a night's sleep before he flew back to Boston, but he had claimed he needed to get back immediately. No, Kenan definitely wasn't comfortable around her. That much was obvious.

She glanced at the tiny clock on her desk and pushed her chair back. What was the use of rehashing the Boston trip? She hadn't had so much as a telephone call from Kenan or Sam in the week since she'd come home. She felt a certain degree of regret that her grandfather hadn't been in contact. Kenan, she could understand, but not Sam. She had cared enough about the fact that they were related to establish a relationship. Had he satisfied his conscience with one meeting?

Oh well, as Mommy Jean often said, "No sense worrying over it now."

Sharley walked to the hall closet and opened the door, jumping back as several items tumbled to the floor. Okay, here was an area of her life she could fix. She found the guys out back washing the cars.

"After you finish that, come on inside. That hall closet hasn't been cleaned in years."

"So what's another year?" Devlin asked

playfully.

"Three hundred and sixty-five days," Sharley teased. Devlin groaned, and she flashed him a grin. "Ask a smart question; get a smart answer. I'll get started."

"We'll be right there," Jack said, picking up the bucket of sudsy water. "We're finished here anyway."

Back inside, Sharley hesitated over the daunting task.

"Are you sure you want to do this?" Jack asked, looking around the crowded space.

"This place has got to be the original lost-in-space room," Devlin added.

"I doubt anyone's cleaned in here since Sharley was a kid."

Sharley bent to pick up the things on the floor. "Come on, guys. It's long past time. We can probably toss half of it."

They were a group who rarely worked in silence, and today was no different.

"Tell us about your grandfather's place," Devlin called as he sorted through old papers.

Sharley took out a new trash bag and placed it in the can. "It's incredible. I toured the place the second day I was there while Papa Sam was at work. He's got a Dover country estate, and let me tell you, there's a bit of everything. He even has a gardener.

Puts my yard to shame."

"Oh, come on, Sharley, you know you win the garden club award every year," Jack said. "Mrs. Gloria did a fine job fixing up that place, and you've kept it up real nice."

"Thanks. To tell the truth, his house was way too big. He's got a helipad for that chopper Kenan flies. There's stables with some of the most beautiful horses you've ever seen roaming about in white fences. His pool was fantastic."

Devlin stopped and looked up, "Since when do you swim?"

"Never, but if I had a place like that, I could probably learn. I lounged out by the pool and enjoyed being waited on."

Devlin hefted two of the filled garbage bags and nudged Jack's shoulder as he passed. "I'm surprised she lowered herself to this lowly work."

"Yeah, what should we call you now?" Jack asked.

"Sharley will do just fine."

"So did you like your grandpa?"

Sharley thought about the question, her thoughts going back to the three-day visit. Both she and her grandfather had made an effort to get to know each other better. She was at a loss as to how to catch up on a lifetime within a few days, but they covered a great deal of territory.

The library was her favorite room in the palatial house. The expensive leather furniture was comfortable, and there was a fire to ward off the chill to his old bones, as Sam put it. Briefly Sharley considered she could get used to the living accommodations, but just as quickly she realized she preferred the coziness of the home she'd grown up in.

"So how did the meetings go?" she had asked Sam the second night she was there, after he had apologized again for leaving her on her own.

"Successfully. Kenan probably could have handled them alone, but he's not comfortable with that extent of responsibility."

That surprised Sharley. Kenan struck her as very in command. "How long has he been with you?"

"Over twenty years. Started out as my pilot and then moved along until I made him CEO. He thought I was crazy. I think I got the best end of the deal."

"How so?"

"I've never had an employee with as much ability as Kenan. There's nothing I ask of him that he doesn't give one hundred and fifty percent. Well, maybe one area, but that's not work-related."

Sharley's brows lifted. "Personal, you mean?"

"His salvation. He's important to me so I stay on him. I'm sure one day he'll come to love the Lord. He's been so restless lately that I've been afraid I might lose him. Now he's perturbed about this latest revelation concerning your mother and Jean. I think he sees me as a hypocrite."

"You never told him the truth before?"

Sam shrugged. "I've never told anyone until now."

"Surely he understands that even Christians are not perfect?"

"I never claimed to be — but I was less than honest with him. Chances are I would have taken the secret with me to my grave if I hadn't sent him to Samuels."

Sharley flashed him a reassuring smile. "Kenan loves you and his job. Besides, if he were going to leave, it would have happened about the time you sent him to Samuels. I'm sure he called on the Lord a time or two while he was there."

"Wish I could have seen that," Sam said. "I've never seen him disconcerted. He's always so in charge."

"Not then, he wasn't. Speaking of Kenan, could you give me his home phone number?"

At the speculative look in Sam's eyes, she added, "I need to see what time we're leaving tomorrow. I have business waiting at home."

She had called Devlin and learned old Mrs. Denton had died that afternoon. The family was scheduled to come in and make arrangements the next day. The service would be delayed until some of the kids flew in. Devlin agreed to assist in the choices, but he didn't like to carry out the actual service, so Sharley had promised to be there for the visitation.

After saying good night to Sam, Sharley went upstairs and reached for the receiver. He might not even be home. Her thoughts were confirmed when the answering machine picked up. "Kenan, this is Sharley. . . ."

"I'm here," his voice interrupted.

"Kenan? I thought you weren't home."

"I screen my calls sometimes."

How could anybody just sit there and listen to someone recite a message into one of those stupid machines? "If you don't want to talk to people, why bother with a machine? Why make people think you'll call them back when you don't want to talk to them in the first place?"

"I talk to them. Eventually." He sounded defensive.

"I'm glad I caught you. I checked in and found that I need to be home by tomorrow afternoon."

"Did you tell Sam yet?"

"Yes."

"We'll need to leave early."

"I can make a reservation."

"I'll fly back with you. I have to pick up the chopper anyway." They said their good nights. As she dropped the receiver from her ear, he called her name so softly she almost missed it.

"Yes, Kenan."

"I think Sam's pretty impressed by you."

"I'm glad."

"I was pretty impressed myself. Yesterday, when you asked about my fears about death . . . did you ask as a friend, a mortician, or a psychologist?"

Two and two didn't always equal four, particularly when a person had time to put all sorts of new twists on the situation. Kenan had probably given the matter some thought and decided she was trying to analyze him.

"A friend," she said quickly. "It disturbs me that you're so on edge about death."

"I've seen a lot of it in my life."

"Sam told me about Vietnam." Sharley settled back on the bed, sticking pillows behind her back as she prepared to let Kenan talk as long as he wanted. Most times things just came out of their own accord if a person just took time to listen.

"It was pretty bad. I was lucky. I only had to survive a few months before I got out of there. Fortunately for me, I was all in one piece, even though my head was a little messed up. Sam helped me to come to grips with that. He's quite a man."

Sharley was glad Kenan had found Sam. God had used Sam's selfish decision, she realized with a sense of surprise. Gloria Samuels Montgomery had been more than capable of dealing with what life had given her. Jackson Montgomery and her child had helped. But Kenan might not have survived his return from Vietnam if Sam had not been in Boston to help him.

"I've got to go, Sharley. Someone's at the door."

She wondered if it were the truth — or if the conversation had become too intimate for him to handle and he needed an excuse to get away from the conversation.

"Good night, Kenan. I'll see you in the morning."

She had replaced the receiver and retrieved her nightgown and bedtime necessities. Her life had taken a decidedly odd turn, she mused. In the last few days, she had inherited a grandfather and become attracted to a man who had an almost pathological fear of death. Things couldn't get much weirder than that. Sharley shook her head. She never understood why people thought her career so macabre. It was indispensable, a loving service she performed for people. Something she and other morticians did because families couldn't take care of it themselves.

"Earth to Sharley," Jack said now, waving a hand in front of her face as he broke into her thoughts.

Sharley jumped. "Sorry. The visit was an experience, Jack. I'm still trying to understand why Papa Sam did what he did."

"I'm glad he contacted you. It's good to have family. You two work your problems out and enjoy the relationship."

Jack's words surprised Sharley. He was right on target with what she was feeling.

"Ooh, la la," Devlin said, holding up an intricately beaded, brilliant red dress. "What is this?"

Sharley touched the garment. "I haven't seen this in years."

"Isn't it a bit fancy for funeral wear?"

Sharley glanced at Jack. "You tell him. You were here when it happened."

"That dress has its own history," Jack said with a wide grin. "Made the headlines — FAMILY FEUD COMES TO SAMUELS."

"According to Daddy, it was legendary," Sharley said.

"Come on, guys," Devlin demanded impatiently. "Tell me."

Jack tugged a folding chair from against the wall, ignoring the tumble of items that fell to the floor. "Sadie Meares was well-known in this town. She had twelve kids, and they scattered like leaves in the wind when they grew up. One daughter, Marilyn, never married and lived at home. She was real protective of the old lady.

"When Sadie died, Marilyn decided it was her right to plan the funeral since she was closest to her mother. Marilyn was known for . . . Let's see, what's the best way to say this?"

"Her absolute lack of taste," Sharley suggested.

Jack laughed loudly. "That sums it up fairly accurately. She put together the most outrageous funeral plans I'd ever heard of in all my years with Montgomery-Sloan. She had us looking for white horses and a carriage. Planned to have a marching band and the family walking behind the carriage. Watched too many old movies if you ask me."

"What about the dress?"

"I'm getting to that. Red was her mother's favorite color. Marilyn was a seamstress, and she went out and bought the material, made the dress, and sewed on all them beads. It got crazy when the rest of the family showed up. They argued, vetoed each other's plans, took votes, changed their minds. Finally reached the point that Mr. Montgomery was ready to send them to the next county. Two of the girls got into a cat fight. I thought they were going to scratch each other's eyes out.

"Everything got changed but the red dress. Marilyn called every hour on the hour to ask what her mother was wearing. Anyway, it was decided that the casket would be closed for the ceremony. A couple of the girls asked for a few minutes alone with their mother after the final visitation. We found the dress in the casket room stuffed under a lining a week or so later."

"Did anyone tell Marilyn?"

"Are you kidding? She went to her grave talking about the fabulous dress her mother was buried in. Let's hope she wasn't too surprised when she ran into Mrs. Sadie up in heaven. Never saw so much hugging in all my life as there was at that funeral."

"Man, I missed out on all the good stuff."

"Thank heaven for that," Sharley said. "I don't think I could be as calm and collected as Daddy."

Later that afternoon, Kenan walked into the back room, half dreading what he would find. The sight that met his eyes astounded him.

Sharley knelt by the chair where Devlin was obviously deeply asleep, his snore reverberating about the room. A bottle of liquid shoe polish sat nearby, and she used a feather to tickle his nose. Only after Devlin swatted his face, rubbing his nose and leaving a black streak, did Kenan realize she was up to no good.

"What are you doing?" Kenan realized he was whispering.

Sharley whirled around, wondering if he were real or a conjured-up figment of her imagination. She decided he was real and grinned unabashedly. She dropped the feather and reached for Kenan's hand, pulling him from the room.

"Just having fun. Payback for the balloon."

"He'll know it was you. You left the evidence."

"I *want* him to know it was me. What are you doing here?"

Kenan seated himself in a wingback chair before her desk and crossed one jeaned leg over the other. "Sam sent me to finalize the papers."

"You could have done that by phone." Disappointment surged through her; she had hoped his visit was more personal. "Sam pretty much filled me in on everything he wanted at his office."

"He wants to see you again."

"And old Triple S couldn't pick up the phone and tell me that himself?"

Kenan frowned. "That's no way to refer to your grandfather."

Sharley rolled her eyes, shaking her head at his admonishment. "Well, excuse me if I'm a wee bit ticked at him right now. Besides, he's a stranger, Kenan. There's no instant bonding between people who never spent any time together."

"Isn't there?"

Sharley pinkened at the roguish tone of his voice. There was something almost tangible between the two of them. Sharley felt as though she should be able to reach out and touch the emotion. But it couldn't happen. Emotions were meant to be felt, not touched. Maybe the world would be a better place if a person could see them in a physical sense. Feelings were too transient, too difficult to understand.

"What gives with you two?" Kenan said. "Your attitude doesn't seem very Christian to me."

His words reminded Sharley of the Bible's charge to show her Christianity through actions. Kenan must be royally confused by their behavior. "Sam was never a part of my life. And though I hope he will one day be my very good friend, I don't yet see him as my grandfather. I don't think he sees himself in that role either."

"He doesn't have long left."

Sharley's greenish-brown gaze fixed on him consideringly. Were his words a gambit to gain her sympathy for his dear old friend, or was her grandfather near death? "Sam strikes me as being in pretty fair health. I don't think he's going anywhere anytime soon, and my personal opinion is that we're both getting what we expected out of our relationship. We were curious about each other, and now that the curiosity has been appeased, what's left? Obviously not much, since he can't take time from his busy schedule to call. What do you expect?"

Sharley wondered if she were being too blasé about the matter. Deep inside, she was happy that Sam cared enough to send Kenan. But another part was upset because he didn't care enough to make the contact himself.

"I expect a normal blood relationship. When he goes, Sam has no one else in the world to inherit his estate. You're his granddaughter. You should be the one to fill his shoes."

Sharley doubted she was up to the job. "You've been a son to him for years. He can leave it to you."

"I don't want it."

"Neither do I. Between the money my dad left and my business, I don't do so badly." When Kenan shifted uncomfortably in his chair, Sharley asked, "How long do you suppose you can hide the fact that you don't care for my work?"

He ignored her question. "I don't understand either of you. You're both waiting for the other to make the first contact. If you want to talk to Sam, call him."

"If the old man's conscience hasn't bothered him before now, it's not my job to make it happen. I'm not going to take a chance that he's too busy for me."

"How can you just forget you have a family?"

"Blood doesn't always make it family, Kenan. And I haven't forgotten Sam exists. I'm glad to hear he was impressed by his granddaughter. I'm glad to know he wants to see me again. Unfortunately for us both, I have a business to run, and that business is a few hundred miles from Boston."

"Does it make that much difference?"

He doesn't understand, Sharley realized. Kenan couldn't begin to comprehend her need to belong to this community. Samuels was her home. Montgomery-Sloan was her heritage. "It matters to me."

"You're like your grandfather in more ways than you realize."

Sharley smiled at that and glanced up when Jack stopped in the doorway. "Hey, boss, ready to pop into the back for a cold one?"

Her gaze moved from Jack to Kenan and back. She indicated Kenan's presence with a subtle tilt of her head. Jack frowned and shrugged before making a hasty exit. "Sorry. Standing joke around here."

"Do you people ever tell regular jokes?"

"Sure. Want to hear a few?"

Kenan's hands came up to ward off her efforts. "I just wondered. I'm beginning to think my sense of humor has gone south for the summer."

"People have a tendency to accept death more willingly when you deal with it often."

"I'll take your word for it."

"You put your faith into a machine that carries you miles above the ground every day. Why is it so difficult for you to believe there's nothing to be afraid of here?"

"Give me a chance to mull that over."

"Maybe that's part of the problem," Sharley suggested, her eyebrows lifting in question with the statement. "Chances are you're spending entirely too much time mulling over the situation."

Kenan squirmed in his seat and changed the topic. "How have you been?"

"Pretty good. I spent most of the morning trying to decide on whether or not to replace my vehicles." She lifted two samples. "What do you think? Pearl gray or white?"

"The gray."

"It is elegant," she agreed, looking at it with new interest. "I was considering ordering a hearse and two limos, but on second thought, maybe I'll just order one limo. I can always rent if I need one. No sense in tying up more funds than necessary."

Kenan cleared his throat. "Sharley, there's another reason I'm here." She looked at him curiously, and he continued, "Sam's birthday is in a couple of weeks. He's planning a big bash. He wants you to be his hostess."

What did they expect of her? "What are you? His paid voice? Is it so very inconceivable that he could pick up the phone and tell me this himself? I haven't heard one word from him since we met."

"Don't get angry. He knew I was coming with the paperwork. He just mentioned the idea."

"So, tell him to call me. I'll see if I can fit him and his party into my schedule." Sharley shoved the papers into her desk drawer and slammed it shut. "I do hope he won't be too disappointed if I'm not readily at his beck and call. My job is demanding, too. I'm required to be available twenty-four hours a day. People won't put their dying on hold so I can attend my grandfather's birthday bash."

"I should have known." The words gushed from Kenan's mouth along with a defeated sigh. "Okay, the truth of the matter is, Sam didn't send me here to bring papers. He didn't ask me to ask you to act as his hostess. They were all excuses. Excuses so I could come here and see what it is about you that won't let me forget you exist."

Sharley felt more alert than she had in days. "Now we're getting somewhere. It scares you, doesn't it, Kenan? You don't want to be attracted to the mortician lady."

"Yes, it does, and no, I don't. But that hasn't stopped it from happening. I was scared when you came to Boston, and I'm scared now. I know you're just a flesh and blood woman. I know your work is something that has to be done. Still, I can't see us together, and yet I can't forget you either."

"Why do you want to forget me?"

"Because we're worlds apart."

Finally they were getting to the crux of the matter. Kenan had made more than one admission. "Why don't we go out to lunch? You'd probably be more comfortable talking in a restaurant."

"I'm not sure I want to talk."

"Make up your mind, Kenan. I am what I am. That is not going to change. If you're interested in me, you have to accept my life."

A war waged itself on his expressive face before the words seemed finally ripped from him. "Then I guess we'd better talk."

They went to the barbecue restaurant where they had eaten before. Kenan held Sharley's wooden slat chair for her and then moved around to seat himself at the wooden table. The restaurant lacked the big-city ambience he was used to, but Kenan found himself liking the homey atmosphere. The walls were painted a stark white, and the windows were open to the parking lot, a swatch of fabric across the top their only decoration. The walls contained painted pictures, tiny price tags tucked in the corner. The owners obviously collected pigs, and some of the pieces were fascinating.

Sharley removed the menus from behind the napkin dispenser and passed him one. A young waitress in shorts and a T-shirt took their orders.

"How do you deal with your job?" Kenan asked. "Those people . . . they're just so . . ." He shrugged. "Dead."

"Good thing. A living person might question my efforts to embalm them."

Kenan grimaced, and Sharley shrugged and grinned. "You accept it as a part of living. Everyone dies, Kenan. And when they do, I carry out their family's wishes. It helps them find peace."

"I've never found anything remotely peaceful about death. My personal history has to do with being six years old and locked in a funeral home for several hours."

"What happened?" Sharley demanded.

Kenan thanked the waitress when she set the plastic cup filled with crushed ice and tea before him. "My maternal grandfather died, and my mom took me to my first visitation. It was fun for the most part — a big place with plenty of places to play with my cousins while the adults sat around and talked.

"There were two things that bothered me. One was when my grandmother clutched my grandfather in her arms and sobbed out her grief. Then my mom touched his face and cried softly, saying how cold he was. I wanted to see for myself so I sneaked a hand over into the coffin. He *was* cold, and I was upset because he made my grandmother and mother cry. I decided then and there I didn't want anything to do with this death business.

"Later, I told my cousins how cold he was, and the older ones started telling ghost stories. I was scared and tired so I found a small room with a sofa and lay down.

"When I woke, it was very dark and the building was empty. For whatever reason, I had been left behind. As an adult I can see how easy it would be to lose one child in so many, but as a little boy I felt deserted. Mom assumed I was with my cousins, and my cousins assumed I was with my mother.

"I was afraid to move from the sofa. I kept calling for Mom until I started hearing strange noises. I got real quiet then because I was afraid my grandfather would come after me." Kenan shrugged. "My cousins' stories really did a number on me."

"No wonder you don't like funeral homes. How long were you there?"

"Four or five hours. It seemed like forever."

Sharley's hand covered his. "You must have been terrified."

"Terrified is a mild word for what I was. I didn't sleep with the lights off for months. My parents argued a lot about that. Dad told my mom she was babying me too much."

"But you were just a little boy."

"Not in my dad's eyes. When he was away, I was the man of the house. I was expected to take care of my mother and sisters. I haven't been to a funeral since."

The conversation halted when the waitress delivered two paper plates piled high with barbecue, coleslaw, french fries, and hush puppies. Kenan wasn't sure he could handle the man-sized plate he had ordered.

"And yet you flew the choppers that transported victims. How did you deal with that?"

"I told myself I was a man. That I could handle it. That my dad would be disappointed if I let him down. I pumped myself up, cajoled, belittled, anything I had to do to get myself through. It was pretty bad, but I guess I was lucky. I only had to survive a few months before I got out of there. Fortunately for me, I was all in one piece, even though my head wasn't the same as it had been before." He shook his head. "I can't explain the feeling that swamps me when I think about death."

"Mainly fear?"

"Yes."

Sharley offered a sympathetic smile. "That was a smart answer on your part."

"It was a coward's answer."

"No, it's not. Only by admitting to a fear can you learn to live with it. As long as you avoid dealing with it, the fear grows and consumes you more each day."

Their gazes locked. "This is not the conversation I planned to have with you."

Sharley chuckled and admitted, "It's not one I thought we'd have, Kenan. I find myself attracted to you, but I know we're going nowhere as long as you're overwhelmed by this fear of what I do for a living."

"How can you prepare a body?" he blurted. "What kind of emotions allow you to deal with someone who once lived and loved just like you?" Sharley saw him shudder.

"How does a surgeon operate on a human being?" she countered. "Is what I do really so different from that? Except for the fact that I don't have to worry about losing my patient on the table, that is." When her smile received no answer, she turned serious. "Truthfully it's no picnic. I've reconstructed accident and suicide victims so that family members could have a final viewing. And this may strike you as gruesome, but I'm as proud of what I've accomplished as an artist is of his paintings. I believe in the business. I'm also not your ordinary undertaker."

That caught his attention. "In what way?"

"I often rush into things. I'm aggressive. I have millions of ideas, and I love a challenge. I like to be the center of attention. I like to socialize. I try to be diplomatic, but I have a temper. I get furious when people think I can't do the same job my father did because I'm a woman."

"I didn't know," Kenan said, recalling how he'd asked for the manager that first day.

"I realize that, but it's a preconceived notion I've been fighting for years." Sharley speared a chunk of the succulent pork and put it in her mouth. She swallowed and said, "Humility and anger aren't a very good combination. People expect me to be staid and respectable. It's not in my genetic makeup to fade into the woodwork. I have to work hard at it. My dad passed up a lot of things he wanted to try in life because he felt they weren't proper activities for a mortician.

"Personally I feel that life is too short not to experience everything one can. I see people every day who will never have the opportunity to try the things they missed. I've performed funerals for stillborn babies, for children, and for teenagers. Those touch me the most deeply. When a seventy- or eighty-year-old comes through my doors, at least I can think, 'Here's someone who has had a full life.' "

She thoughtfully sipped her iced tea. "I suffer for the bereaved, too. That's another reason why I have to do my best. I want them to have what it takes to help them live in peace with their losses. It's not a money thing. But when all is said and done, it becomes something you do. A job." Sharley broke off as an idea occurred to her. "Maybe if you actually saw what goes on . . ."

Kenan shook his head, dread filling his eyes.

"Maybe not," Sharley agreed. He wasn't ready for that step. First, he had to get past his fear of death. Then maybe he could understand that preparation and burial were the logical conclusions. "I wish I knew the magic words that would make you more comfortable, but there aren't any. Besides, I told you once I was concerned as a friend. I don't think we'd get very far if you kept thinking I was trying to analyze you."

Kenan picked up the check the waitress laid on the table and escorted Sharley to the checkout. He paid, and they walked out to his rental car.

"Did you want to come back to my house for coffee?"

"I was hoping for a repeat on the room offer you made last week," he admitted with a grin. "I didn't think to make arrangements for somewhere to stay. The B and B is full."

Sharley hesitated. "After what we've just discussed, do you think it's wise?"

"I have no dishonorable intentions, Sharley," Kenan said quickly. "I need a place to sleep. I'll take you up on that cup of coffee, and we'll talk some more. I could tell you about the Sam I know."

"I'd like that."

The sun was dropping fast over the horizon as they neared the town's flashing caution light. Kenan's gaze caught on a flurry of political posters for seats on the board of education, sheriff, state and congressional representatives, and, of course, coroner.

"So that's your political aspiration. Nice poster."

Sharley glanced over at him. "Thanks. Samuels is located in one of the few North Carolina counties where coroner is an elected position." She noticed his expression. "Somebody has to do it, Kenan. I'm qualified."

Silence eased back into the car as they turned up Montgomery Street toward her house.

"You don't have to do this if you don't want to," Kenan said.

"It's okay. The house is full of guest rooms."

"Will my staying over compromise you in any way?"

Sharley smiled and shook her head. "My great-aunt Liza happens to be spending some time with me. She goes to bed early, so you won't meet her tonight, but she's the perfect chaperone."

Kenan climbed out and went around to remove his flight bag from the trunk. "Lead on, Ms. Montgomery."

Sharley showed him inside the house. "Let me show you where you'll be sleeping, and then I'll pour us a couple of glasses of iced tea. We'll take it out onto the patio. It's too nice a night to stay cooped up inside."

She left Kenan to change and came back downstairs.

"Sharley?" he called a few minutes later.

"In here."

He followed her voice into the neat kitchen. Sharley's eyes lingered on the muscular forearms exposed by the shirt. "How do you keep up your regime when you're traveling?"

"I generally try to stay in hotels with fitness centers."

"You certainly have an admirable physique."

"I could say the same of you," Kenan returned, grinning at her bold compliment.

She laughed. "There's a weight machine in the basement if you're interested. Dad and I used to do a few reps now and then."

Kenan poked her upper arm. "Oh ho, another bodybuilder."

"Not exactly. I haven't been near the thing in months. Daddy needed it for muscle tone, and I encouraged him. You're welcome to use it."

"I might just take you up on it later."

Sharley led the way through the utility room, stopping long enough to retrieve cushions for the chaise lounges. They made themselves comfortable, and she tilted her head to stare at the full moon. The unlit area glowed with its eerie but iridescent light.

"Hard to believe it'll be pitch-black dark out here in just a couple of nights," he mused.

"Full moons bring out strange behavior in some people."

"Even in small towns?"

"Particularly in small towns," Sharley pointed out. "So tell me about the plans for this gala affair for Sam."

"Just an intimate party with a few hundred of his closest friends." Sharley heard the tinkle of ice against glass as Kenan took a sip of tea.

"He'll be eighty?"

"Yes. How old was your mother when she died?"

"Sixty."

"So Sam was a father at eighteen?"

"That sounds about right. That would have made him a grandfather at forty-five." Sharley felt too lazy to attempt the mental math and shrugged her shoulders. "How did you end up in Vietnam?"

"Family tradition. Dad was retired Air Force. He wanted his only son to have a military career, but I refused to allow him to rule my life. I graduated at seventeen, got in a couple of years of college, and joined the army. They gave me more flight training and made me a warrant officer pilot. I ended up on a chopper in Nam. I learned very quickly that the only career I wanted had nothing to do with the military."

"Do you have a lot of bad memories?"

"Every Nam vet has at least one good nightmare. I was scared. It wasn't a matter of waltzing into a combat zone and doing cleanup. The medevac choppers are crewed by a pilot, copilot, two gunners, and two medics. We evacuated the wounded, usually from hot fire zones. We'd move into the zone, machine guns blazing, and the medics jumped out with the stretchers. It was my job to get us in and out. Some guys got high with excitement, but I always felt I was playing Russian roulette with a fully loaded gun. From what my friends told me, I was better off in the air than on the ground. Still, I experienced a lot of things I could have lived my life without."

He fell silent, and Sharley knew he had said more than he intended. She changed the subject. "So tell me the story of how Sam made his fortune in Boston. He didn't take a lot with him when he left."

"Sam has always been a visionary," Kenan said. "He worked hard and made his first million marketing items for inventors. He kept investing and backing new ideas and built up a group of loyal followers. People who invented regularly and were interested in him marketing their product. It was a workable relationship for everyone."

"Why did he have to go to Boston to do that?"

"Sam told me his father didn't care much for change. When he worked in the bank, his dad wasn't interested in anything but a sure bet."

"Most bankers aren't."

"Most bankers aren't Sam Samuels. Every time he approached his father with some innovative technique he was sure would make a difference, he was told, 'That's not the way we do things.' He stood it for as long as he could, and then one day he packed up his bags and left. Unfortunately it appears he left his wife and child behind."

Maybe Sam had the right idea, Sharley thought, *at least financially.* The First National Bank of Samuels had merged into a larger banking system long before she came into adulthood.

"So maybe if his dad had been more flexible, Papa Sam would have stayed in town?"

"Possibly. It's hard to imagine, though."

Sharley nodded, not realizing that Kenan couldn't see her in the dark. "What about his personal life? Did he remarry? Do I share him with other grandchildren?"

"Sam once told me he wasn't cut out to be a husband. Over the years, he escorted women here and there, but he never committed to anyone else. And while I'd love to tell you everything I know about Sam, there are things he shared in confidence that I would never be able to tell you."

Sharley smiled. "I can respect that. I've prayed a lot over this situation. As a child, I was the focal point of my parents' lives, and I couldn't understand why my grandfather Samuels treated Mom as he did. It didn't matter when Mom told me it was okay. I held a grudge. Then I grew up, and I became a Christian. Forgive and forget became part of my life. I'm being tested now. Am I the Christian I want to be? Maybe. I have to be sure I'm not being hypocritical. It's not about Papa Sam making up the past to me. It's about our making a future with the time we have now."

"Well, I can understand the hypocrite part."

The dryness in his tone caught Sharley's attention. "What do you mean?"

"Forget it."

Like a dog worrying a bone, Sharley

asked, "What's on your mind, Kenan?"

"I'm just trying to reconcile this new truth about Sam with the man I thought he was. He's always going on about Jesus, and then I find out he deserted his family. That's not something a Christian does, is it?"

"It's something a confused Christian might do," Sharley pointed out. "Or something that someone might have done before he became a Christian. Our God is a forgiving God. He forgives us when we do things that are wrong."

"Well, I don't know much about that, but you should see him when he tells people about his beautiful granddaughter. Sam particularly likes to tell them you're an undertaker. Most of the staff were as shocked as I was. They had no idea. He loves to tell them you call him Papa Sam and you're as alike as two peas in a pod."

Sharley found it interesting that Kenan didn't want to discuss the matter further. "I wouldn't go that far," she said softly. "My friends have been shocked by the news. Maybe I can get him to come for a visit. There aren't a lot of his generation left, but there are probably people who remember him."

"Sam doesn't travel much, Sharley. The trips to and from the office are about the extent of his excursions."

"I see."

"You seem disappointed."

"No, just confused. Tell me, Kenan, does Sam really want me to act as his hostess, or was it an excuse?"

"Sam's talked about you all week. He's impressed by his granddaughter, but he is dealing with his pride. I don't think he's ever come to grips with what he did to his family. He justifies it by telling himself they were better off — but he missed them, too." Kenan sighed. "No, Sam didn't send me here. But he does hope you'll be his hostess."

Sharley looked thoughtfully up at the sky for a moment, and then she got to her feet. "It's getting late. We'd better call it a night. You probably want to get an early start tomorrow."

"We haven't discussed us yet, Sharley."

She turned to look at him. "Is there a future Mrs. Montgomery in Boston, Kenan?"

"I was involved with a woman until just before my vacation. We were good friends. I felt we had enough going for us to make a good marriage."

"She didn't agree?"

"Jocelyn didn't want a marriage based on

friendship. She feels we deserve the fireworks."

"I see. Do you see these fireworks as part of our relationship?"

"There have already been a few explosions." He chuckled, and she found herself liking the sound.

"I'm nothing if not voluble, but my fuse isn't that short. What about our differences, Kenan? The potential problems we might face?"

"I'm not thinking about them right now."

"So I'd be a diversion?"

"I'm ready to settle down. Eager to find the right woman and start a family. Why are you running for coroner?"

"It's something I want to do."

"Isn't your job gruesome enough without you being called to heaven only knows where to look at all kinds of horrible sights?"

"This is a small town, Kenan," she said, a small measure of exasperation in her tone. "We rarely have anything more involved than someone slipping away peacefully in their sleep. Granted, old age may be considered gruesome by some, but it happens to us all sooner or later."

"And how do you feel about this thing that's happened with us?"

"I'm as curious as you are, but I'm not

packing to move to Boston. I'm praying about it."

Kenan sprang to his feet and paced restlessly. *And that pretty much says it all,* Sharley thought. She sighed. "As I said, it's late. Let's just sleep on this."

Sharley went into her room next to Aunt Liza's and listened to the sound of the shower and then heard his door click shut. Kenan Montgomery fascinated her. In some ways, he was everything she wanted in a man, and more — and she surely was getting impatient for a husband.

She slipped into her nightgown and picked up a brush, sweeping it through the curls. So what did she think about his readiness for commitment? She was ready to find the right man and settle down to married life and babies herself, but she had her doubts that she and Kenan could ever be right for each other. Not if his life wasn't committed to Christ.

Kenan stepped from the shower and toweled dry, taking care to pick up after himself. At home he might not have bothered, but for some reason he didn't want Sharley thinking he was a total slob.

He had surprised himself with the overwhelming urge to see her again, but he had hated to admit to her that his visit had absolutely nothing to do with Sam Samuels and his birthday. It was an excuse and a sorry one at that. He should have just told Sharley he wanted to see her again and left it at that. Now he had her upset because Sam hadn't taken the time to call and invite her to the party.

Sam would probably rip into him for that one. He knew Sam and Sharley were negotiating the most complicated contract of all, and now he'd botched it up miserably. No way she'd believe now that Sam was calling because he wanted to. Not unless he made her understand.

Kenan pulled on a pair of sweats and the shirt he'd worn earlier and stepped into the hallway, searching for an indication of where Sharley's room was located. He spotted the light underneath the doorway on the other side of her aunt's room. He tapped and listened for sounds of stirring. She might have drifted off and left her light on. No, he could hear the muffled volume of the television, the nightly news.

Sharley was belting her robe when she opened the door. "Kenan, what is it? Is something wrong? Did you need something?"

Now that he had her full attention, Kenan

didn't know where to start. The truth was always the best place. "First off, I need to apologize."

"Apologize?" Tiny lines of confusion crinkled her forehead.

"For not telling you why I came. I misled you into believing that Sam sent me. He doesn't even know I'm here, nor was it his intent that I invite you to the party. He told me yesterday that he planned to call and issue the invitation this weekend. I jumped the gun because I wanted an excuse to see you. I needed to see you."

"Needed to see me?"

Kenan nodded. "We might have some major differences of opinion on a variety of topics, but attraction has an agenda of its own. The heart doesn't always figure the differences into the equation. It just knows that something is right, and I can certainly tell you my heart is pretty impressed."

Her eyes were swimming, he saw. Maybe he wasn't doing such a good job here.

"Thank you, Kenan. That was so beautiful."

He reached for her hand. "I don't want you upset with Sam for something that isn't his fault. I should have told you the truth from the start. See, you're already having a good influence on me."

Sharley laughed.

"Now get some sleep," he said, leaning to kiss her forehead. "I'll see you in the morning."

Long after she returned to bed, Sharley lay thinking of what he had said and wondering what hope there was for the future.

"Lord, I believe You have a plan for me that You will one day make clear. Help me be patient and receptive to Your wishes when that day comes."

Chapter 5

A week later, Sharley adjusted her body against the strings of the hammock and smiled her satisfaction at having a Saturday afternoon free to enjoy such a beautiful setting. The yard overflowed with flowers planted by generations of Montgomery women. Old-fashioned wild roses; pink, purple, and white Formosa azaleas; white baby's breath; and a pink dogwood were just a few of the bounty of blossoms.

The daffodils had already shown their sunny little faces, and Sharley looked forward to seeing her personal favorite, the irises. Gladiolus, lilies, and a multitude of others would follow. She pushed the feeling she should be working in the garden far back and felt little remorse. The sun shone brightly, the sky was a clear blue, and the air was redolent with the odor of the grass that had been cut the previous day.

The only thing she could think of to make

it better was Kenan. *Kenan,* she thought dreamily. Her eyelids drifted closed with the lazy sway of her string cradle in the spring breezes, her thoughts on the man who had happened into her life.

He had left town early the previous Sunday morning. Sharley insisted he stay for breakfast and meet Aunt Liza. Her mother's best friend had come to visit for a few days, and the three of them had talked more over eggs, toast, and coffee.

Her relationship with God kept Sharley thinking that to pursue a romance now with Kenan would mean being unequally yoked together — but she couldn't help but hope that one day Kenan would find Christ and things would be different for them both.

She had no idea when she would see him again. No doubt a religious mortician gave him plenty of room for dilemma.

Kenan's eyes were drawn to the tiny smile at the corner of Sharley's mouth. Her devil smile, he called it, noting its frequent appearance, particularly when she was in a playful mood.

He had meant to surprise her but instead he found himself surprised. Her business was locked up tight, and she was here, resting peacefully in her backyard. He hated to wake her, but their time together would be limited as it was.

The fragile stem of the flower snapped beneath his hand, and he moved to tease Sharley awake. A gentle brush across her nose resulted in a wrinkle and a frown. Her hand rose at the second sweep, and Kenan's lips replaced the flower with the third.

Her eyes opened wide as he locked his fingers in the mesh fabric and lifted playfully. "You're looking entirely too comfortable."

"Kenan. You're here," Sharley cried. He let go, and the hammock swayed softly.

"In the flesh." One long finger tapped the book that lay open against her chest. "Boring?"

Sharley lay back, feeling at a slight disadvantage as she looked up at him. "I didn't hear a chopper."

"It's in Boston. Sam didn't send me so I couldn't take advantage of his good nature. I caught a flight and rented a car."

"But you drove for two hours. Why didn't you call?"

"If I'd known business was so slow, I would have."

"No funerals this week."

"You mean you've had the entire weekend off?" Kenan asked. He could have flown up earlier and spent more time with her.

"Yes, but I had to stay close to home. You never know."

Deathwatch, Kenan thought grimly. He wouldn't let the thought spoil their time together. He was here, and they were going to be happy. "You never answered my question about the book."

"Definitely not boring. It's my grandmother's journal. I know more about Papa Sam's parents than I ever did. Mommy Jean lived next door to the Samuelses when she was growing up, and from what I've read, spent almost as much time at Stewart and Catherine Samuels's as she did at home."

"Sounds like quite a discovery."

"Oh, it is. Can you believe it? She's written about my great-grandparents, Papa Sam's parents."

"You seem excited."

"Well, it is another part of my life I didn't know. And a different side of my grandmother. Her mother died when she was an infant. My great-grandfather never remarried."

"Why haven't you read the journals before?"

"When Mommy Jean was alive, it seemed an invasion of her privacy. I don't think Mother ever read them."

"Have you read the part where she and Sam fell in love?"

Sharley smiled at the thought Kenan was as intrigued by Sam and Jean's romance as she was.

"For the longest time, I think she was more in love with his parents. In the part I'm reading now, she's at that age where young Sam is a real pain, but they're on the verge."

On the verge. Just where their own relationship teetered.

"I just ran across this entry. Listen. 'Sam noticed me for the first time today. For my sixteenth birthday, his mom brought me a grown-up dress and helped me put my hair up. When I took my regular seat in the Sunday school class, he actually smiled and waved, even though he was with a bunch of his pals. It was wonderful. Then he came over and sat with me during the sermon and afterward asked if he could walk me home. I said okay since we were both going that way anyway. Mary Beth Langley didn't like it one bit. She's so sure Sam will marry her, but she need not be because one day I plan to marry him.' " Sharley reread the name, trying to place the woman. "Mrs. Hinson and Papa Sam?" she exclaimed in disbelief. She laughed outright. "I can't imagine that peppery old lady and Papa Sam together."

"Go on. Does she say how she managed it?"

" 'He lingered for a while until Daddy announced it was time for lunch and told Sam he'd better get home before his father came looking for him,' " Sharley read. " 'Daddy's such an old grouch at times. I don't know why he couldn't have invited Sam to stay.' "

Sharley laughed. "That's not what she said when I was sixteen and interested in a boy."

"No encouragement?"

"None whatsoever."

Kenan bent to examine the hammock. "Will this thing hold two people?"

"It's supposed to."

"Slide over. I suddenly feel the urge to be lazy."

Kenan lay beside her, keeping one foot on the ground. They hung at an angle; Sharley rolled up against him.

"Come on, Kenan. Lift your other leg. We aren't going to tip over."

He relaxed, and they rested together in the webbed enclosure.

"How's Triple S?" Sharley chuckled at his quick frown. "You're determined he and I will adore each other, aren't you?"

"I'd like to see you accept your grandfather."

"He called me last week. Wants me to come up for his birthday party."

"Will you? It could be his last birthday."

A jolt of dismay shot through Sharley at the thought. She didn't want to lose her grandfather. "Let's hope not. Besides, can you imagine what some of his guests would think? Not only a surprise granddaughter, but a mortician."

"Are you worried about what they would think?"

"Not particularly."

"Sam gets a real kick from telling his friends his granddaughter is an undertaker."

"I'd prefer mortician or funeral director." They shared a smile. "I plan to visit Sam again. Just as soon as I get my life in order."

"What about becoming coroner? You'll have even less time and more demands on the time you do have."

"I'll find a way. I always do. Does he know you're in Samuels?"

"No."

"Why? It's not his place to approve or disapprove of our getting to know each other."

"I can't say that. He's my friend. The fact that he's related to you makes it doubly hard to keep it between us."

"Why does it have to be a secret?" Sharley

asked finally.

"Because I don't want to get his hopes up. I'm afraid Sam would push us if he knew."

"Maybe so." Sharley gave him a skeptical glance.

"You don't believe me?"

"Oh, I believe Sam might push you. But I was wondering if you were reluctant to talk to him about your own attraction. You have to admit you aren't exactly delighted with the way things have been happening between us," Sharley said.

They lay in total silence, each contemplating the words.

"So, how's the historical research going?" Kenan asked finally.

"Nothing new on the town, but lots of interesting reading on our family. These journals are memoirs. Mommy Jean covered every little detail. There's a lot about their childhood years. Her family were Reynoldses. They moved here when she was eight, and her father bought the local hardware store."

"You won't find anything like those journals in our family. I doubt my dad could tell you his great-grandfather's name."

"Too bad Papa Sam can't attend the celebration," Sharley said thoughtfully.

"Don't suggest it to Sam, Sharley. He'd send me as his representative." Kenan flashed her a lopsided grin.

Sharley smiled back. "So how was your week?"

"Extremely busy."

"And you jumped on a plane and came here rather than resting over the weekend? I wish you had called."

Kenan wondered about the regret in her tone. "What are your plans for the rest of the day?"

"Strictly politics. I've got to get out on the campaign trail later on to shake some hands and kiss some babies."

"Do you really do that? Kiss babies," he supplied at her questioning look.

Sharley grinned. "I can't resist most of them. If I'd known you were coming, I would have scheduled this for another time or at least gotten some volunteers to take my place."

"Sounds as if you're already too busy for me. But if you need volunteers, I'm good with a hammer and a stapler."

"Never let it be said the Montgomery Campaign for Coroner turned down a pair of willing hands."

Two hours later Kenan's feet ached and he

forced a smile. He stopped thinking of Samuels as a small town at the end of the first hour. He was on intimate terms with every intersection and had a passing acquaintance with all the places a person could rest their weary body.

"Stop frowning, Kenan. You're scaring away my supporters."

He wasn't having fun. He'd walked alongside Sharley, growing more perturbed when their conversation was frequently interrupted by her stops to shake hands and distribute campaign literature.

"You don't have to do this," Sharley said at his long-suffering expression.

"I don't mind."

Her laughter trilled around them. "Like you don't mind a root canal."

Kenan caught her hand in his. "I came to see you. If this is the only way I can see you, I'll deal with it. Meanwhile, I'll help in any way possible."

"In that case, I'll let you take this future coroner out to dinner after we finish. I know just the place."

"Pretty confident, aren't we?"

"Why not? I go after the things I want. Mr. Jones," she called and moved to talk with the potential supporter.

Things she wanted, Kenan thought as he

waited for her to finish her conversation. Did he fall in that category? *Obviously not.* If he had called, Sharley would have given him a million reasons why he shouldn't make the trip.

In his heart, Kenan knew the biggest reason was fear. No doubt his hot and cold behavior confused her as much as it did him. Probably explained why she constantly reminded him of the distance that separated them.

Maybe she was right. He felt like he was beating his head against a brick wall. The situation seemed pretty hopeless. Sharley's life was entrenched in Samuels. He doubted she took time from her busy campaign schedule to think about him.

She returned, and they continued to walk. "Tell me about the dinner everyone keeps mentioning," he said.

"The church holds fellowship dinners. The members invite their friends to break bread with the congregation. We don't have to go if you think you would be uncomfortable."

Before he could answer, a young woman pushing a baby stroller hailed them. Kenan smiled when the baby lifted her arms toward Sharley, indicating that she wanted to be held.

Sharley handed him the flyers. The mother

nodded her okay, and Sharley leaned down to unsnap the restraining lap belt. "How's my girl?" she asked.

The toddler jabbered some nonsensical language that contained one understandable word: Sharley.

"Kenan Montgomery, this is my friend, Beth Thompson, and her daughter, Claire. Where's my other girl?"

"Welcome to Samuels," Beth said to Kenan before turning back to answer Sharley's question. "With her daddy. A group of men started practice for a T-ball league. That's where we're headed now. To see Cindy play."

A wistful smile touched Sharley's face. "Oh, I bet they're too cute for words."

"It's interesting," Beth said, grinning broadly. "Cindy and the others haven't quite grasped the concept of team sport."

"Cindy's in my Sunday school class," Sharley told Kenan. "Maybe we'll stop by after we finish."

"Cindy would love to have Ms. Sharley in the stands rooting for her. Of course, she'd probably rather sit in your lap than play ball."

"Give me some sugar, Claire?" Sharley coaxed. The baby allowed her cheek to be kissed and was all smiles when Sharley returned her to the stroller. "I'll be rooting for Cindy."

"Don't show too much enthusiasm. Dan is looking for sponsors for the team." When Sharley laughed, Beth said, "Hey, I'm serious. These guys are getting so desperate they'd take the funeral home's money in a heartbeat."

"How many of my other kids are playing?"

"At least four."

"That's enough for me. Tell Dan he's got a sponsor if he's interested."

"You don't have to, Sharley."

"Sure I do. I want my little darlings to be as well dressed as the other teams. Just tell Dan not to make the uniforms dark and let's keep the funeral home name low profile and dignified."

They waved the mother and child off, and Kenan asked, "Why did you do that?"

"It's a few dollars for a good cause. These children aren't exposed to a lot of extracurricular activities, and it doesn't hurt me any to help where I can."

"Do they all know what a generous person you are?"

"Afraid so. Let me take some of that stuff," Sharley offered.

"I'm balanced. Lead on, Ms. Montgomery." Kenan found himself shifting the items until he could take Sharley's hand in his. "I imagine the town is a far cry from the one Sam knew."

"Not really. Some things have changed. The bank doesn't have the Samuels name associated with it. The Reynolds family no longer own the hardware store. There are a few new businesses and less old ones. More cars on the street. A few less people in the population count."

When they passed a church, Sharley drew to a halt at the gate. "Here's something you might like to see."

Kenan eyed the cemetery and said, "Not particularly."

"Oh, come on. It's where Sam will be buried. My mom and grandmother are here, along with Sam's parents."

The cemetery was well kept with monuments dating back to Samuels's beginning. Sharley pointed out various ancestors.

"You don't have to go far to shake your family tree. Appears they're all right here."

"My tree is down to a branch."

"Don't worry. You'll give it new roots."

"I hope to."

"How many miles do you plan to walk today? My feet are killing me."

"Oh, you. We'd better get moving. We're losing daylight here."

■ ■ ■ ■

Later, while dressing for dinner, the situation between Kenan and herself overwhelmed Sharley's thoughts. She cared deeply for Kenan, but if he was right with Christ, her own life was important, too. Certain things, the family business and even her political career, had been a part of her life plan for as long as she could recall. Reconciling Kenan's place in her life seemed impossible.

She thought about it often, sometimes telling herself that once he had a living relationship with God, all they would need to be happy would be for him to give up his life and move to Samuels. And then she would shake her head at herself, for that was about as realistic as Santa, the Easter bunny, and the tooth fairy all rolled into one. Kenan enjoyed his job with her grandfather. She enjoyed her life in Samuels. And the miles separating the two made it highly unlikely either of them would find common ground.

Kenan couldn't cover the distance that separated them forever. Still, she did something she'd learned to do a long time ago and put it into the Lord's hands. The doorbell rang, and she glanced in the mirror one last time. Kenan was here to take her to dinner.

"You're looking mighty handsome," she said, taking in the sight of him in jeans and a casual shirt. "There will be a gleam in several sets of mothers' and daughters' eyes tonight."

"Too bad. There's only one Samuelite I'm interested in."

Kenan drove them to the church in his rental car. Sharley led the way inside and introduced him around the room. One of the town's oldest citizens sat in her usual place of honor. "Who have you got here, Sharley?"

"Mrs. Hinson, this is Kenan Montgomery. He works with my grandfather in Boston."

The old woman's piercing eyes pinpointed Kenan. "So you work with Samuel?"

"Yes, ma'am."

"Mrs. Hinson," Sharley said, "I ran across your name in Grandmother's journal. You never told me you dated my grandfather. You know we recently met for the first time?"

"I imagine Jean didn't say much that was good. That was many years before I met my Billy. Of course, if I had married Sam Samuels, he'd never have gone traipsing off to

Boston."

"Oh, I don't know, Mrs. Hinson. I get the impression nothing would have kept him in Samuels."

"It was your grandmother's fault. She wasn't woman enough to keep her man by her side. All her highfalutin ways, thinking she was better than everybody else."

Sharley bit back her temper. "I'll be sure and tell Papa Sam I met one of his old sweethearts next time we talk."

"Don't matter one way or another to me. Never did hold much to him running off and deserting his family. God blessed me with a much better man."

Sharley almost snorted her disdain. Billy Hinson barely had two pennies to rub together all his life. He had lived off his wife's family for as long as Sharley had been alive. Of course, Mary Beth Langley had been an old maid when she met Billy Ray Hinson, and chances were she'd given up on marriage.

"Forgive me, Lord," Sharley whispered, realizing she was being judgmental. She couldn't help but think how everyone's life could have changed if her grandparents had never met. Especially hers. If Sam Samuels had chosen this woman as his wife, she would not have existed.

"It's been nice talking to you, Mrs. Hinson."

"You tell Sam I still think he did wrong."

"Persistent, isn't she?" Kenan held Sharley's hand as she pulled him through the crowd. "Is that the one we read about this morning?"

"I imagine she was more his type at sixteen. The years have a way of changing people."

"Maybe she's one of the reasons he left. I wonder how many more feel like she does?"

"Most men and women in this town don't take kindly to someone being done wrong, Kenan. But they are Christian enough to forgive and forget when someone does make a mistake. If Papa Sam came here, he'd be welcomed as befits his status as descendant of the founding father. No questions asked. Come on, let's fix ourselves a plate."

Kenan followed Sharley through the line, and they joined a table of her friends. She introduced him around and then joined the chatter. A young man stopped by the table and rested his hands on Sharley's shoulders. She looked up at him, and her face blossomed into a pleased smile.

"Pastor George, this is Kenan Montgomery. Kenan, this is our pastor, George Roberts."

"Glad to have you with us, Kenan."

"Good to be here, sir."

"Call me George. Perhaps we can talk a bit later. Enjoy yourselves."

"Isn't he a bit young to be a pastor?" Kenan whispered after the reverend had moved on to another table.

"He's the best, stomps on toes, wakes people up, and everyone still loves him. His wife's a real sweetie, too. You'd better finish that if you want seconds. The food at these dinners disappears fast."

Sharley's popularity was even more obvious as she chatted with the various people who made a point of searching her out. Kenan gave up when the team coach claimed her attention.

"Beth said you were willing to be a team sponsor."

"Don't sound so eager, or I might be tempted to put stipulations on my sponsorship."

"Sharley honey, we're so desperate that if you insisted on glow-in-the-dark skeletons and calling the team 'Dem Bones,' we'd take you up on it."

Sharley laughed in delight. "Hmm. Scare the competition away. Now that's tempting, but I think the objective is to make our little darlings look as good as the other team. It's bad enough that they have to have Montgomery-Sloan on their uniforms at all. Maybe I should just make a private contribution."

"After all you've done for this community, we'd be proud to wear your name on our uniforms."

Kenan wandered over to the dessert table. He took a serving of lemon pie and was about to take a second for Sharley when Pastor George came to stand beside him.

"Kenan, right?"

"Yes, sir."

"Please call me George."

Kenan smiled politely, but he wasn't comfortable with calling a man of the cloth by his first name.

"We have a larger group than normal tonight," the pastor said. "I'm glad you could come with Sharley. Remind me where you're from."

"Boston. I work with Sharley's grandfather."

The pastor smiled. "That certainly was a surprise. And where do you attend church?"

"I get to the Baptist church near my home occasionally."

"Easter and Christmas?"

Kenan was startled by the man's bluntness. He was embarrassed to admit the pastor was right.

"I see. So are you a Christian?"

"I believe in Christ. I suppose I haven't been all that faithful about serving Him."

"Believing is half the battle, Kenan. Serving Him is important, too. Sharley would be the first to tell you that. She's one of our best workers in the church. I've come to know her even better since we conducted several funeral services together and can honestly say she has a steadfast devotion to the Lord. And that's what really counts — a living relationship with the Person of Christ."

What was this man trying to tell him? Kenan wondered as he glanced over at the table where Sharley sat. "From what I know about Sharley, she does everything with gusto. Seems only natural she'd give her all to her church, as well."

"So true. I'd say she's given her all to God as well. It's been good talking to you. I'll remember you in my prayers."

Kenan muttered his thanks and escaped the uncomfortable ordeal, his mind spinning with the pastor's words. Was Christianity like a badge you wore for the world to see? True, he'd always been told a true believer was known by his actions, but he'd done nothing here tonight to indicate he wasn't a Christian. So why had the pastor buttonholed him this way? And yet strangely enough, these people accepted him into their group, without demand that the sinner leave their presence.

Kenan wandered back to the table, passing Sharley the pie. She told him about the team's escapades. A number of the little team players stopped by to hug Ms. Sharley and to tell her they would see her in Sunday school. *She's good with children,* Kenan thought as she pulled another one onto her lap and teased him into a big smile.

The time slipped by, and before either of them realized it, most of the food had been packed away and the cleanup process was well underway. Kenan helped Sharley pick up the few plates and cups that dotted the tabletops and tossed them in the trash.

"We'd better get you over to the B and B before they lock up for the night."

Kenan negotiated the way to Sharley's house with relative ease and caught himself thinking of how long the same trip would have taken in Boston.

"What are your plans for in the morning?" she asked him.

"Nothing really," he said. "I've got a flight out in the afternoon around four, but I'm free until then. What did you have in mind?"

"I thought you might want to go to church with me."

"I don't have suitable clothes." An excuse. Years ago when his mother had made him attend Sunday school, he learned you always wore your best. Of course he did have a pair of dress slacks and a little dressier sport shirt.

"It was just a thought. You seemed to get along well with Pastor George. I thought you might like to hear him preach."

"Do you ever miss church?"

"Rarely. My week feels incomplete when I do."

"So you wouldn't consider taking off to be with me?"

"God never takes a day off, Kenan. The least I can do is spend a couple of hours in His house. Besides, my little ones will expect their Sunday school lesson. You're welcome to come with me. No one would mind if you wore your jeans."

"I could treat you to lunch afterward."

When she didn't make a comment right away, Kenan realized Sharley was disappointed.

"I'd like that," she said at last.

The following day they lunched at the bed-

and-breakfast restaurant. Sharley met him there after church, and they spent an enjoyable hour together. "This place has good food," he commented.

"Martha does know how to cook," Sharley agreed. "She could open a restaurant if she didn't like the B and B better."

He rolled his arm to look at his watch and sighed. "Time for me to hit the road if I plan to make my flight."

"I'm glad you came."

Kenan didn't respond. He picked up the check and stopped by the cashier to pay before ushering Sharley to her car. He bent and looked in the open window. "What if I asked you to give my world a try? I've come to Samuels and spent time doing the things you do. Will you do the same for me?"

Sharley stared into the dark depths of his gaze. "It's impossible. I have commitments. I can't just pack up and go running off to Boston. Besides my business, I have my Sunday school class and my campaign. May is closer than you realize."

"So, I'm not worth the effort. Everything is more important than me?"

She sighed her exasperation. "I didn't say that."

"I've put everything in my life on hold for the past two weekends. I've had work to do, places to go, people to see, but you were important enough for me to decide I should come. I guess I know where I stand."

"Don't give me that, Kenan Montgomery. If it had been really inconvenient, you wouldn't have come. You've surprised me both times, so it wasn't a planned thing. Just maybe in the back of your mind you thought, 'I'll pursue this thing with Sharley' — but it wasn't an anticipated, planned trip."

"I did anticipate seeing you again," Kenan growled. "That's what this is all about. I don't plan my life anymore. Mostly life happens — and we happened. So now, what are we going to do about it?"

"You tell me."

"You really want to know what I think?" Kenan asked, anger simmering deep in the black gaze. "No, I don't think you do. I know your entire family was so caught up in proving Sam made a mistake in leaving Samuels that you would never consider wanting a life elsewhere."

"That's not true. I have traditional values that include pride in my hometown. I would never desert Samuels."

"Finish your sentence."

"What do you mean?"

"The unspoken 'like my grandfather

deserted his town.' You claim you don't harbor any resentment, but deep inside you do. You've taken on your heritage like a burden. This is a community, not a dictatorship. You're not mayor or a member of the city council. You're just a prominent businesswoman in the community. I think you're running for coroner to get a political in."

"That's not why."

"Then why?"

"Because I'm qualified. My sense of civic duty is strong. I want to be important to Samuels."

"You want to be recorded in the annals of history?"

"I want my kids to have a sense of belonging."

Her words hit Kenan with all the force of a kick in the stomach. "A sense of belonging," he repeated slowly. He could understand that.

His father had been in the military, and as a child, he had moved frequently until his father left the military and used the land his parents left him to open a flight school. Kenan was ten, and the idea of staying in one place forever excited him. No more transient friends. He loved everything about Texas and flying. It was as close to perfect as he thought life could get. And then Vietnam destroyed all that. By the time he returned home, his world was too out of whack for him to live there.

Kenan stared at her for a minute longer before he said, "I've got a plane to catch."

Chapter 6

"This is too unreal," Sharley whispered, looking out the window as the plane circled Logan International.

"Did you say something?"

She glanced at the man who had traveled from North Carolina in the seat next to hers and shook her head. "Just thinking out loud."

Sharley couldn't believe she was doing this. Sam and Kenan had no idea she was coming to the party. She had just decided herself this morning after the two huge flower arrangements arrived, one from Sam, the other from Kenan. She wasn't looking for excuses, but she had to acknowledge that this was one of the few remaining birthdays she would share with her grandfather.

Her attempts at resuming life as normal failed miserably. She filled every waking hour with Montgomery-Sloan, politicking, church activities, and any social event she could cram in, but the unfinished business with Kenan and Papa Sam lingered, refusing to allow her to forget.

Every time she considered their conversations, she told herself that she was better off without either of them — but her emotions were telling her the complete opposite. Kenan had made an impact on her in more ways than she wanted to consider.

She read the journals and contemplated how it must have been for her grandparents when they were in love. The truth that she, too, wanted to be in love weighed even heavier. Sharley sensed her emotions could easily grow, but she refused to give consideration to Kenan's terms. And anyway, until he drew closer to the Lord, she couldn't even consider pursuing their relationship.

For her birthday, the guys had taken her out to breakfast and presented her with a beautiful cake. *Too beautiful.* She insisted they have a slice, and the moment the knife touched the luscious frosting, it exploded in a boom of confetti and frosting.

Jack and Devlin had all but rolled on the floor laughing. The lack of business gave them more opportunity to laugh and gloat, and finally Sharley left them to their merriment and went to her office.

She picked up the fax from the machine

to find it was from Sam. It was a birthday greeting of sorts, filled with wishes for a wonderful day. He had penned a note reminding her the scheduled date of the party was that night and he'd love to have her there.

And since no business commitments stood in her way, she packed her bag and made her reservations. Jack and Devlin thought it was a great idea. Jack volunteered to drive her to the airport, and Devlin ran by the dry cleaners to pick up her dress. Sharley knew subconsciously she must have all along wanted to attend because she had taken her best evening gown to the cleaners on Monday.

Kenan's most recent visit was all the impetus she needed. She was drawn to him, and though she prayed constantly for God's guidance in the matter, she understood exactly where Kenan was coming from when he spoke of the heart being involved. In a very short time, she had grown exceedingly fond of him. Actually she knew her feelings had gone far beyond fondness, and while they might not be full-fledged love, they were something very close.

"Do you think I'm doing the right thing, Jack?" she asked, just minutes before leaving for the airport.

"I think that if you don't go and see what it is you're missing, one day you'll be sorry."

"Hey, boss, got your dress here," Devlin yelled. "Jim put it in the garment bag and stuffed it with tissue to keep it from wrinkling. Better get a move on if you want to catch that plane. This dress is going to impress your new boyfriend."

"Kenan's not my boyfriend."

"Sure he's not," Devlin said.

"Haven't seen anyone so moony-eyed since Devlin's lady said yes to his proposal," Jack teased.

They weren't far off with their teasing. "You guys are crazy."

"Crazy like a fox. You can't fool us. Your grandfather may be in Boston, but someone else is there, too."

She couldn't lie. Not even the anger she had felt after Kenan's accusation changed her feelings. They hadn't talked since he'd left Samuels, but she hoped to discuss the matter while she was in Boston. He deserved the same chances he'd given her.

The plane touched down, and Sharley retrieved her carry-on bag and the garment bag holding her dress. Outside the airport, she hailed a cab and directed the driver to take her to the hotel. She needed to call Kenan and ask if he would mind giving her a lift to the party.

Would Sam be surprised? Sharley thought so, despite his persistence. The note had been only one of the reminders he'd sent; most of them had been closer to demands that Sharley act as his hostess. She had refused repeatedly before he finally accepted her decision. Last time they spoke on the phone, he said he understood. They chatted for a few minutes longer, and he suggested they get together soon. Sharley promised to make every effort to schedule another trip to Boston.

After checking in, Sharley went directly to the phone and called the number on the card Kenan had given her. His instructions had been to call anytime she needed to get in touch with him. *Now would be one of those times,* she thought as she waited for his secretary to answer. What was Kenan going to think about her change of plans? She gave her name, and the secretary transferred her without hesitation.

"Sharley? Is something wrong?"

"Everything's fine. I'm here in Boston. At a hotel. I decided to surprise Papa Sam."

"He'll be delighted, but why didn't you go to the house?"

"Surprises are generally more effective when the person being surprised doesn't know he's being surprised," Sharley pointed out.

"Fine. Sam will be happy. He was disappointed that you couldn't come."

"I need your help."

"How so?"

"I couldn't find Sam's house if you offered me a million dollars, and I suspect it's a steep fare for a taxi."

"Why don't you call and have Jamie pick you up?"

"I could do that," she agreed, trying not to show the disappointment she felt at his words. "I just thought you might like to take me to the party. Sorry to have bothered you. I'll see you later."

What had happened? The chill in his voice was enough to give her frostbite. Maybe he was still angry because she hadn't agreed right away when he asked her to come to the party.

She started to say good-bye, but he interrupted her. "Sharley, wait. I'd love to be your escort. Can you be ready by six?"

"Are you sure, Kenan?"

"Positive."

"Then I'll be ready and waiting."

"See you shortly."

Sharley hung up the phone and glanced at her watch. There was time to grab a bite to eat before she dressed. She went downstairs to the restaurant.

Five-star certainly didn't have anything to do with their restaurant service, Sharley decided almost forty-five minutes later when her meal arrived. Her plenty of time had been cut by almost an hour. She'd be doing good to have showered by the time Kenan arrived. He was going to be upset. Oh well, she could always tell him to go on and call Jamie as he'd suggested.

Kenan hesitated outside Sharley's room door and listened to the sounds coming from inside. *Why is she laughing?* he wondered as Sharley's uproarious laughter drifted out into the hallway. He knocked loudly enough to be heard.

The door opened, and he stopped short at the sight of her in a long satin gown, holding what looked like a formal red dress.

"What's so funny?"

"Those guys are a riot. Read this."

Kenan didn't have to ask which guys. What had they done now? He took the paper and read aloud, " 'Thought you might like a new dress for this formal occasion.' "

"I had Devlin pick up my dry cleaning because I was running late," she explained.

"I must be missing something here."

"Look," Sharley said, flipping the beautifully beaded red gown. "They've given new meaning to the term backless."

Puzzlement creased Kenan's face as he fingered the fine fabric of the dress.

"It's a shroud, Kenan. Funeral clothing. They must have switched it after he picked up my dress."

He dropped the fabric as though it were red-hot.

"Wonder what Triple S would think if I showed up in that?"

"What were they thinking?" Kenan exploded. "Doesn't it bother you in the least that these guys have pretty much stopped you from attending the party? You can't go with your entire back exposed."

"It's no big deal, Kenan. I can probably pick up something in one of the shops downstairs."

"Sam's guests will expect to find his granddaughter attired for the occasion."

"Haute couture? Well, then they would have known the gown I intended to wear was off the rack, wouldn't they? So, tell me, what do I wear to Sam's party?"

"You should fire those guys."

"I know beyond a shadow of a doubt that something backfired. They wouldn't have intentionally left me without a dress. Besides, how can I fire them for something I started? Our jokes bring fun into the back rooms, and no one gets hurt."

Kenan felt his cheeks redden as he recalled his reaction at their first meeting.

"Well, not usually," Sharley said. "That time with you was the exception." She touched his face. "There's no reason to be ashamed. We did agree no customers in the future. I was afraid you would sue me."

"I suppose we could call a few shops and see what we can find. Or . . ." Kenan began, breaking off as he realized Sharley probably wouldn't care for the idea.

"Or what?"

"There's a woman I know. She's about your size. Has a lot of formal clothing."

"How do you know what's in her closet?" Sharley asked.

Kenan refused to meet her gaze. "We, ah . . . we . . ."

"Spit it out."

"It's the woman I used to date. Jocelyn."

"And it doesn't bother you to ask a favor of her?"

"Well . . . no," he admitted. "We had an amicable enough parting. You need a dress, and she has enough gowns to outfit her own shop. I'm sure she has something more appropriate than we can find on such short notice."

"Don't just stand there. Call her."

Sharley watched Kenan walk across the room. The sight of him in the black tuxedo took her breath away. She'd never known a man who could look so at home in a monkey suit, as her dad called a tuxedo. As he spoke on the phone with the other woman, one part of her wanted to be jealous that there had been someone in his life, but another part knew she had no right to feel anything.

"She'll wait for us," he said as he hung up the phone.

"Wait? Kenan, are we interrupting her plans?"

"She has a function. All the more reason for you to throw on something, and let's drive over right now. She lives in my building."

"I'll get dressed."

Minutes later, Kenan was tapping on an elegant door in an expensive high-rise condominium. The doorman had cast a doubtful look at her when she entered with Kenan. No doubt he found her wanting when it came to Kenan's usual companions. She had to admit she did look like she couldn't make up her mind: Her denim jumper was a bad match for the hair, makeup, and silver pumps.

The door opened, and Kenan said, "Jocelyn Kennedy, this is Charlotte Montgomery, Sam's granddaughter."

"Ms. Montgomery, I'm so pleased to meet you."

"Sharley, please. I can't tell you how thankful I am for your help."

Jocelyn Kennedy was dressed in a gown that made Sharley's original choice look like a bargain basement treasure. Her dress matched the beautifully decorated home, and yet Sharley felt comfortable with this woman who was certainly upwardly mobile career-wise to have achieved so much in her life. Or maybe she came from a wealthy family as well.

"I nearly died when I found that dress," Sharley said, launching into a description that soon had the other woman fighting tears of laughter.

"That's priceless," Jocelyn whispered, wiping her eyes. "Let's go take a look in my closet. Actually I should let you see if you can wear this one." She waved at the dress she had on. "It's new and none of the guests will have seen it before."

"Absolutely not," Sharley said. "I'm sure you have something that will suit me just fine without taking the clothes off your back."

Jocelyn looked doubtful. "But everyone will expect Sam's granddaughter to . . ." She trailed off.

Sharley laughed. "Kenan and I just had this conversation. The first thing people will have to learn about Sam's granddaughter is not to expect the expected. I'm certain any gown you loan me will be more appropriate than the one I left in my hotel room."

They left Kenan in the living room, and Sharley followed Jocelyn through her beautifully decorated bedroom into a dressing room the size of her bedroom at home. One entire section was devoted to evening gowns. "Let me think for a second. Some of these wouldn't suit your coloring." Jocelyn sorted through them quickly before pulling one out. "Try this. I have no idea why I let myself be talked into buying it in the first place. It really doesn't suit me."

"Obviously so you could loan it to me," Sharley said as she quickly slipped her jumper off and reached for the emerald green satin dress. It was the most beautiful thing she had ever seen, exactly the type of dress she would have chosen.

She stepped into the gown and pulled it in place. It was a perfect fit. "I think we've found the dress."

"You're easy to please," Jocelyn said, smiling as she zipped the dress. "But I must admit it never looked that good on me."

Sharley glanced over her shoulder into the mirror. "I know better than that. You've saved the day, Jocelyn. I hope we haven't ruined your plans for the evening."

"Don't worry. I canceled."

Sharley's groan of dismay sounded throughout the room.

"Really, it's not a problem. It was more of an obligation than anything else, and I told the hostess an emergency had arisen. You'd better go before you're late. Kenan's probably wearing a hole in my carpet. I've never seen him so overwrought."

Sharley looked into the mirror and reached to tuck a loose strand into the neat upswept hair style. "Do you see a lot of each other?"

"Are you asking if we're involved?"

Sharley nodded.

"He's a friend. Kenan helped me through a rough period of my life." Jocelyn reached for a tissue. "I was jilted. He let me borrow a shoulder. He wasn't dating anyone then either."

"I wouldn't blame you if you had feelings for him," Sharley said, watching Jocelyn in the mirror. "He's quite something."

"He's a wonderful man, but there's nothing there for us. Now, let's get you to the party."

Sharley did a whirl as she stepped into the living room. "So, what do you think? Isn't this better than a shroud?"

He gave her a once-over. "Much better."

"You're an absolute lifesaver, Jocelyn," Sharley repeated.

"Glad I could help. What about your guys and the dress?"

"Could I borrow your phone?" Sharley dialed Jack's home number. "Hello, Jack. Thought I'd check in and see if you and Devlin were running my business into the ground?"

She caught Kenan's grimace out of the corner of her eye and winked at Jocelyn when she giggled. Sharley placed a hand over the receiver and whispered, "Kenan hates our funeral home jokes."

"It's quieter than a tomb around here," Jack said. "How are things in Boston?"

"Not good. The backless dress you and Devlin slipped in on me isn't going to go over well with my grandfather."

Silence greeted her words. "Didn't you get the other one? Devlin sent it special delivery."

"Where?"

"To your grandfather's."

"Since he doesn't know I'm in town, I bet he wonders why my dress is over there."

"Sharley, I'm sorry."

"That and a dollar will get me a cup of coffee, Jack. I owe you big-time for this one."

"Retribution doesn't become you, boss."

"Oh, I'm not harboring a grudge, but I will get even. You'd do well to remember that warning. Kenan thinks I should fire you both, but I think I'll keep you around to torment."

"You could change once you get there," Jack suggested.

"Maybe. Meanwhile I suggest you let Devlin know I said no more tricks with my wardrobe. You've caused a lot of trouble. Good night." Sharley replaced the receiver and grinned at Kenan and Jocelyn. "He's dialing Devlin's number right now."

"This is pretty bad," Kenan said.

"Not as bad as the time they had a mock paper made up with my obituary. I did a double take at breakfast that morning."

"What other kinds of jokes have they pulled?" Jocelyn asked.

"There was the time they set up my entire office under a tent in the parking lot. I just sat there until they tired of that one. Then there was the time they left a note for me to call Mr. Fox, and when I called, I got the zoo. They wrapped my favorite coffee mug in cellophane, and I poured coffee all over the table without getting a drop in the cup. The list goes on and on. Oh, we're going to be late. Jocelyn, since we ruined your plans, why don't you come with us? It's a dinner buffet so one more won't hurt. Besides, you're already dressed for a party."

"I couldn't. It wouldn't look right," Jocelyn said quickly.

"It's better if she doesn't," Kenan agreed.

"Sure you can. You know everybody." Sharley watched as Kenan and Jocelyn shared looks of surprise. "You're afraid it might be uncomfortable?"

"Well, yes. Kenan and I did see each other for some time."

"Which means my grandfather is well acquainted with you, and I'm certain he would love to have you attend. Besides, I'm indebted to you, and if you don't come, I won't enjoy my evening. Not to mention, there are bound to be eligible men at this party, and no beautiful woman should ever pass up the opportunity to meet handsome, wealthy men."

"Sharley." Kenan's voice held a note of

warning.

She flashed Kenan a stubborn look. "Well, she is available. Can't you introduce her to some nice men?"

"Deliver me from matchmakers," Kenan all but shouted.

"It's okay," Jocelyn said softly. "Sharley's right. I'd like to find the same thing you've found."

Sharley looked at Kenan. "No, it's not like that," she said. Kenan echoed her words.

"If you say so. Mr. Right could be at that party tonight, and not only would I miss him, but I'd also spoil your evening."

"Exactly. Now grab your coat, and let's surprise Papa Sam."

The party was everything Sharley imagined, and more. Her grandfather appeared both pleased and surprised by her arrival and insisted that she join him in the receiving line. The next hour became a whirlwind of new names and faces. She hoped there wasn't a test later, for she couldn't recall any of them.

Just when Sharley wasn't sure whether her feet or legs would give out first, the line diminished. Papa Sam led the way to a grouping of comfortable chairs. "A concession for my old age," he said as he settled in one and indicated Sharley should do the same. "Now, when did you arrive? Where is your luggage?"

She named the hotel. "I got in this afternoon. I wanted to surprise you, so I called Kenan and invited myself along."

"You should have called me. I suppose I should be grateful that you're not staying with him."

"What do you mean by that? Kenan doesn't deserve that. He's been nothing less than a gentleman."

"Maybe not, but I'm not a blind old man either. I know mutual attraction when I see it. He's a striking young man. Perhaps you're flattered by his interest?"

"And if I were?"

"I don't want you making a mistake."

"And would Kenan be a mistake?"

"You deserve someone who is as close to the Lord as you are. And I can't help but think of my own marriage. My problems with Jean weren't about love. They had to do with our lifestyle. She refused to bend. She wanted to live and die in a small town. I didn't. If either of us had been willing to change, chances are we would have stayed together."

Like herself and Kenan: They couldn't agree on lifestyles either. He would never be content to live in what he called a one-horse town, and she was too steeped in tradition to give it up. Was Sam trying to warn her?

"Kenan's a lot like me," the old man said. "I pray every day that he'll come straight with God — but even when he does, he likes it here. He has a future with the company. I don't see him giving it up. Now on the other hand, if you came to Boston . . ."

"It's not going to happen," she said softly. "Kenan knows my reasons. He's been to Samuels a couple of times. I know he considers you a friend and is afraid you'll disapprove of our relationship."

"There's nothing I'd like better than to see the two of you together. That is, if you were more evenly matched."

Sharley was beginning to hate that phrase. "You're right about the attraction. Kenan asked me to come to Boston. Your birthday party was an excellent excuse, but he's the main reason I'm here. I know I must wait until God shows me the man He wants in my life, but I'm drawn to Kenan like a moth to flame. I just need to make sure I don't get singed."

Sam laughed. "We all get a little crisp around the edges in our search for God's companion for us. Heaven knows I've tried, but for reasons known only to him, Kenan has refused to open himself to God. I play on his good nature all the time, asking him to accompany me to church. I can tell he sometimes wants to refuse, but my frailty has served as an excuse many times over."

Sharley's wry smile was indication of her own guilt. "I took him to a church social last Saturday night. But I don't think force-feeding him religion is going to do the trick."

"Perhaps not, but I think maybe you're the person who can help him understand God's plan for him."

"Kenan and I are dealing with an attraction right now, but I seriously doubt it will ever get to the point where our differences will be an issue."

"Never underestimate the power of love, Sharley."

"I exercise a great deal of caution in terms of my physical needs."

"Sharley! That wasn't what I meant."

"Yes, it was. And don't sound so shocked. God gave me those desires, and He will lead me to the man He wants to share my life and father my children. That's just one of the areas I place in His hands. I refuse to attempt to second-guess Him."

"Then perhaps Kenan Montgomery isn't

that man. So stay away from the fire."

"How can you be so sure, Papa Sam? God brought me to you. Maybe God sent Kenan to me."

"Think, Sharley. You're here tonight with one of his old flames. Get to know him first."

"If it weren't for that old flame, I'd either not be present or woefully underdressed for this crowd." She told him the story of the practical joke that had gone awry.

Her grandfather shook his head. "If you'd called, I could have had a selection of gowns here in a matter of minutes."

Sharley didn't tell him her gown was probably somewhere in the house. She just shook her head. "I think you're missing the point. It's because of Jocelyn that I'm here dressed as I am, and because of me, she's here. She had other plans, which she canceled to help me out. I'm in her debt."

"Then I'm indebted as well."

"As you should be." Sharley slipped her shoes off and massaged her aching toes. "I think I'll visit the buffet. Can I get you anything?" She stood, wiggling her toes in the deep pile of the Oriental rug.

"Sharley, put your shoes back on immediately."

"You aren't ashamed of your country

bumpkin granddaughter, are you?"

Sam leaned his head back against the chair and stared at her. "No, my dear, tonight you're a very beautiful reminisce of the wonderful times I had with Jean. You look very like her, as did your mother in those photographs you shared. Thank you for taking the time to send them to me."

"You're welcome. Mommy Jean and Mother were class acts."

"She would have fitted in well here," Sam said softly. "If only she had been willing to try."

He seemed miles away, and Sharley offered no response. She could only agree that her grandmother would have been an asset to Sam's world. A class act from the top of her elegant head to the bottoms of her well-shod feet, Jean Samuels always knew the right things to say and do, a trait Sharley wished she had inherited.

"So tell me, did you bring your old grandfather a gift?"

"I'm not gift enough?" she countered.

"You're a wonderful surprise."

Sharley reached for the small bag that matched her shoes and retrieved an envelope. "Sorry it's not gift wrapped."

Sam slit the seal on the back. He scanned the greeting card and then the enclosed document. A huge grin split his face wide open. The grin was soon followed by guffaws of laughter.

Sharley looked up to find Kenan quickly approaching.

"Kenan," Sam gasped, laughter punctuating his words, "she gave me a funeral for my birthday."

Heads turned all around the room, focusing on Sam as he laughed with abandon.

"Well, it is something I knew you wanted."

"Sharley darling, you're a treasure. Don't ever change," Sam instructed. He gestured for Kenan to come closer and whispered a few words. Kenan disappeared from the room and returned with a small package. Sam placed the box in Sharley's hand, closing her fingers about it. "I want you to have these. They belonged to my mother. There are other pieces I plan to give you as well. Jean insisted I take them when I left. Wouldn't even keep them for Glory."

Sharley snapped the hinged lid open. "They're stunning." Her fingers trembled as she removed the antique pearl earrings from their velvet bed.

Jocelyn moved quickly, resting one hand on Sharley's shoulder. "Why don't we visit the powder room? You can put them on. They'll look wonderful with your dress."

Sharley appreciated the woman's effort to help as a flood of emotion overwhelmed her. "Excellent idea. If you gentlemen will excuse us." As they moved through the guests, Sharley whispered, "Thank you for understanding, Jocelyn."

Jocelyn nodded politely to someone she recognized and flashed Sharley a sympathetic smile. "I remember how I felt when I was given something that belonged to my grandmother."

The ladies' room was almost empty, and Sharley was glad. "It's just that I never had a chance to know her. Now I have something that belonged to her."

Jocelyn hugged her. "Thank you for insisting I come. Kenan didn't think it was a good idea because he was afraid of the gossip, but I don't think he argued the point because it was something you wanted."

"An argument would have been senseless. Thanks to you, I'm here tonight. I'm going to strangle my employees when I get home."

Jocelyn chuckled. "Don't. I can't wait to hear how you get retribution."

"One of them is getting married in a couple of months. What do you think? A backless tux or something really original on the soles of his shoes?"

"Provide the limo and substitute the

hearse."

Sharley broke into laughter. "That's priceless. If I didn't care so much about ruining his bride's day, I would."

"Bring her in on it. Just park the limo around the corner." Jocelyn smiled.

They stepped around the corner, just in time to overhear two women talking.

"What do you think about this granddaughter? Isn't she cute in Jocelyn's cast-offs?"

"With more than one of her castoffs." The catty remark launched them into sniggers of laughter.

Jocelyn looked horrified, and Sharley dropped one eyelid in a wink and lifted her head higher. She wrapped one arm about Jocelyn's and pulled her forward.

"Grandfather is eternally in your debt for loaning me this dress after that fiasco with my gown. He asked about repayment, and I suggested a large donation to your favorite charity. You should be hearing from his office any day now."

Jocelyn almost laughed at the women's gasps. "There's really no need, Sharley."

"Of course there is. Goodness should be rewarded. So, are there any keepers out there tonight?"

Jocelyn caught on quickly. "One guy asked

if he could take me out after he got rid of his date. Said she was in the ladies' room and he could be rid of her in under thirty minutes."

Sharley winked and gave Jocelyn a thumbs-up when the women all but ran back from the room. "That was bad. My mom always told me God doesn't like ugly."

"It wasn't a lie," Jocelyn defended. "One of their dates did ask — and those women weren't being particularly nice."

"True, but I call myself a Christian. Following God does not mean that He doesn't want us to laugh and enjoy life, but I was pushing things pretty far just now."

Jocelyn looked at her thoughtfully, but all she said was, "I see."

Sharley wasn't sure that she did, and she offered up a quick prayer that Jocelyn would find all she herself had found in service to the Lord. She replaced her earrings with her grandmother's and tilted her head from side to side. "What do you think?"

"They're beautiful. Why don't you sit here and admire them for a few minutes? I'll let the men know you'll be back shortly."

Sharley smiled and reached to squeeze Jocelyn's hand. "Thanks."

After Jocelyn left, Sharley reached to touch the earrings that dangled from her lobes. They were valuable, but they were more precious because of their connection to her great-grandmother. Even if he'd used all his considerable funds, Papa Sam couldn't have given her a more priceless gift.

She stood and lifted her purse from the vanity, taking one more look at herself in the designer gown. It wasn't a look she was familiar with. While her clothing wasn't cheap, it was a far cry from this elegant creation. She shrugged. It wasn't something she planned to get used to. There weren't many occasions in Montgomery that warranted the formal wear she already owned, and certainly none where people expected her to wear designer originals.

Sharley rounded the corner and glanced at the small groups that dotted the room. Papa Sam was holding court from his chair. Sharley decided it was a good time to find Kenan, but she didn't see him anywhere. She stepped through the open door onto the terraced patio and looked around. There he was, with Jocelyn. She took a couple of steps and found herself stopping when Jocelyn mentioned her name.

"You've really found a jewel in Sharley."

"Yes, she's wonderful." Kenan's grim acceptance seemed to surprise Jocelyn.

"What's wrong, Kenan?"

"I now know what you meant by fireworks, but our situation is far from perfect."

"Why on earth would you feel that way?"

"Her life is thousands of miles away," Kenan said, sounding discouraged. "Our opportunities to be together are so limited."

"But surely now that she's found her grandfather, she'll consider coming here."

Kenan shook his head. "Sharley and Sam don't know each other well enough for her to take that step. Besides, she's developed roots to that place that go all the way to China. Her business has passed through generations of Montgomerys to her. She won't let anyone else have control."

"Still, if the flames burn high enough, you'll change for each other. Nothing stands in the way of people who truly love each other."

"You'd be surprised at the walls between Sharley and myself."

Sharley felt a childish urge to stamp her foot and demand they stop discussing her. Why couldn't Kenan understand there was no one else to take over Montgomery-Sloan? She was it, the end of the line, all there was. Perhaps if she'd had other siblings the situation would have been different. She might have been free to leave her life in Samuels — but she wasn't. She couldn't even think of a way to communicate the importance of what she had to do to Kenan.

Sharley charged forward. "Enjoying yourselves?"

Jocelyn turned and smiled. "I've never had so much fun at one of Sam's parties."

"It's quite an affair," Sharley agreed. "Of course, you could fit most of the population of Samuels in this house. The crowd literally leaves me breathless. I need to walk in the garden. A breath of fresh air and some time to enjoy this glorious moonlight might just revive me."

"I'll go with you," Kenan said.

"Are you sure you should?" Sharley asked, glad he couldn't see her face in the dimly lit area. "Morticians are used to darkness. They deal with it more than other mortals."

"Aren't morticians normal mortals?" he asked.

"I like to think we're as human as the rest, but a lot of people seem to think we're not quite normal." Even as the words left her lips, Sharley knew the best way to handle things was to get through this party and go home to Samuels. Back to the people who understood her.

"Everything okay?" Jocelyn asked.

"The emotions are under control," she said, forced cheerfulness in her tone. "I do love these earrings."

"Sam has a portrait of your great-grandmother wearing them."

"Oh, I saw it before," Sharley said, realization dawning. "I didn't know who she was. I'll have to take another look."

"Why don't we do it now?" Kenan suggested, taking her hand in his.

"No, you two go ahead with your conversation," Sharley insisted. "I can go alone."

"I want to show you," Kenan insisted. "Coming, Jocelyn?"

"Thanks, but I've seen it."

Kenan led the way up a wide staircase that would have done the most majestic Southern mansion proud. Once more Sharley was struck by the fact that this place was literally a palace. The gallery was an extra-wide hallway showcasing Sam's art collection. Numerous artistic renderings by famous and not-so-famous names lined both sides of the wall.

"Sam's gallery reflects his personal tastes and not what some gallery owner says it should," Kenan pointed out.

Sharley turned on her heel in a complete circle and nodded. "I like most of what I see here."

"There's the painting."

She stood before the picture of the woman

who had given birth to her grandfather. "She's beautiful."

Kenan nodded. "From what I can understand, this is another of the items Sam brought from Samuels. Your great-grandfather gave her the pearls for their twenty-fifth anniversary and had the painting done."

For a moment, Sharley was almost angry that Mommy Jean had so effectively cut her off from the Samuels side of her family. She could have kept the painting and the jewelry for her mother and herself, as a memento of Papa Sam.

"Are you glad you came?" Kenan asked as Sharley moved slowly along the area.

She stopped and turned to face him. "Not particularly. Tonight has certainly been eye-opening. I overheard your conversation with Jocelyn just now."

"Does it bother you that I was in the garden with her?"

"Not as much as it does that you'd discuss things with her that you haven't shared with me."

"We're old friends. Tell me what's upsetting you."

"There's nothing bothering me beyond the fact that I didn't use the sense of a gnat before making the decision to fly here. It's not exactly been ideal, has it? You weren't pleased by my surprise appearance. Then there was the debacle with the dress. And my insisting that Jocelyn accompany us even though you both felt it would be uncomfortable. Tonight has been reinforcement after reinforcement that we're not right for each other. I already knew, but then I met Jocelyn and got a good look at the kind of woman who interests you. I like her very much, but I could never be like her, Kenan."

"I wouldn't want you to be."

"Papa Sam pointed out that you and I don't really know each other. We both know it would never work. I've even heard the words from your own lips. Don't deny it. I arrived in time to hear you voice your doubts to Jocelyn."

"I'm sorry, Sharley. She's a good friend. I've always been able to talk to her about anything." He shoved his fingers through his hair and gave her a sideways glance. "So, what do we do?"

"We concentrate on a friendship rather than a relationship. When you call now and then because Papa Sam asks you to, I'll greet you politely and ask how things are. You find the woman who's right for your world, and I wait for the man God intends to share mine."

"God can't intend you to have another man," Kenan growled. "Why would He put us together and allow these feelings to grow if it weren't His intention that we share something?"

"Perhaps we should give the devil his due. Maybe he's tempting us. Probably he wants to confuse you even more about God."

Kenan gave her a skeptical glance. "So what's the devil trying to do to you?"

"He's testing my commitment to the Lord."

"Is that all we are? A temptation to each other?" Kenan moved forward and slipped his arms about her. His face loomed closer, and his warm lips touched hers. The kiss went on until finally Sharley wriggled from his hold.

They stood silently for a moment while their breathing slowly returned to normal. "I'm sorry, but my feelings run more deeply than that," Kenan snapped. "I'm tempted, okay. Tempted to see if I can stomach life in a little one-horse town to be closer to the woman I love."

The consequences of her actions hit Sharley hard. She'd been claiming God was in control, but in her usual controlling manner she was prompting Him with answers to her own questions. And just as surely as she drew her next breath she was in love with Kenan Montgomery. A deep, irrevocable love that would serve no purpose beyond the heartbreak of them both.

"Well, don't just stand there," Kenan complained. "Say something."

"It's exactly as you said," Sharley managed finally. "We care about each other, but the obstacles are insurmountable. There's no way you can understand where I'm coming from on the matter of Samuels."

"Why couldn't you come to Boston? Sam's here. And me." *And I love you,* Kenan admitted to himself. Since the day he had first laid eyes on Sharley Montgomery, his heart had been trying to tell him something.

"It's not that easy, Kenan. You just can't understand how anyone can claim to love somebody and just walk away, can you?"

"Can you?" he demanded, taking a step forward. "If I remember correctly, you never claimed to understand Sam's reasons for leaving your grandmother and mother. Why would you want to do the same all these years later?" Kenan's face was serious. "Think about it, Sharley. You say there's only a blood bond between you and Sam, but no real emotional tie. Both of you want a relationship but don't really pursue one. Sam, probably because of guilt," he guessed, shrugging his shoulders. "Your reasons go a little deeper. Maybe fear of being hurt — but then there's loyalty to your mother and grandmother. And yes, I know you're a Christian, but that doesn't mean you're any less likely to be hurt if things don't work out. I think you've been guarding your heart."

"You think you have me figured out, don't you?"

"Close enough."

"I'd say it's possible you missed your calling. You're right about most of that — but there's still the fact that though Sam and I may be related we're still strangers."

"Nonsense."

"Why are you trying to turn this around on me? I wasn't even born when Triple S made his decision."

"But your mother was, and I can imagine your grandmother told the story often."

"You don't know anything about my family," she protested. "Maybe I am too committed to Samuels. I know and love those people. Every year I see the population shrinking when young people go off to better-paying jobs while Sam Samuels runs a multimillion-dollar corporation in a city hundreds of miles away. Think what that business would have done for Samuels. He could have turned the town into a thriving metropolis."

"It wouldn't be the same place, Sharley. More people, more crime. More of the undesirable elements than you can imagine."

"I could accept that more easily than I can its turning into a ghost town."

"Why don't you just say it?"

"Say what?" Sharley demanded, exasperated by the way he had turned this situation on her.

"That you could never love me as much as you love Samuels?"

What had she done? Things were totally out of control. One moment Kenan was telling her he loved her, and the next moment they were attacking each other. She took a deep breath and said coolly, "Since you're so intent that Papa Sam and I bond, I'm going back to the party. He'll wonder what happened to me."

She walked slowly toward the stairs, her feet dragging as she wondered if each movement took her away from Kenan for the last time.

"Sharley, don't do this. Please, not now."

She glanced over her shoulder. His agony impacted her as nothing ever had before. She couldn't run fast or far enough to escape the gut-wrenching pain that filled her. "Good-bye, Kenan."

"Sharley."

Don't look back. She repeated the words like a silent litany, trying to convince herself it was for the best. Tears welled in her eyes, and she knew her mascara wouldn't survive the trip downstairs.

Back in her grandfather's presence, Sharley was drawn into a conversation with the group of people who now surrounded him. She had no idea how much time had passed and only spoke when her grandfather prompted her with a question. Once, as though he knew what she was feeling, Papa Sam reached for her hand and patted it gently.

He spoke softly, and she leaned down to catch his words. "Will you stay here for the rest of your visit?"

Sharley nodded, certain she couldn't get words past the lump in her throat.

"I'll send Jamie to pick up your bags."

"Perhaps I should go with him. I left the room in rather a mess, and I need to settle the account."

"I'll send someone to help him, and he can take care of the account."

"Okay," Sharley agreed simply. There was no fight left in her. "I need to tell Kenan."

Sam handled things quickly, and the conversation promptly picked back up. Sharley noted Kenan standing with Jocelyn on the fringes of the crowd that had gathered about them and refused to meet his eyes. She couldn't make herself tell him of her change in plans. Not yet.

It was almost midnight when he approached her. "We should be going."

"I think it best if I stay here with Papa Sam for the next couple of days. He's already sent someone to pick up my things so I won't trouble you again."

He looked like he wanted to say something but didn't.

"Thank Jocelyn for me, please."

"Thank her yourself," he snapped before turning away.

Sharley bowed her head and whispered a small prayer for Kenan's comfort.

How could she do this to them, to him? Kenan wondered. And for what? A business and a town? A sense of belonging? He had never felt this way until Sharley had walked into his life. For the first time, he was truly in love.

His life had been in turmoil since Vietnam. He'd made some strides over the years, buying the condo, his first real home;

deciding he was ready for marriage and a family was another step in the right direction, even though Jocelyn refused him.

Thank God for that, he thought now. He would have been miserable with her after meeting Sharley. But why had the Lord put Sharley in his life only to tear them apart? She could pretend there was nothing between them, but in his heart, Kenan knew his feelings for her had moved beyond friendship.

"Sharley's not coming with us?" Jocelyn asked.

He looked at her and sighed. "No, she's staying here with Sam and her God."

"Kenan?"

He shook his head sadly, unable to look her in the eye. "I'm sorry. That was uncalled for."

She touched his arm. "It'll be okay."

"I'm glad you think so because I'm not so sure."

"She loves you, and believe it or not, Charlotte Montgomery is going to be worth everything you have to do to bring her into your life."

"She wants my soul."

"No, Kenan," Jocelyn corrected. "She wants you to give that to God. Maybe it's time we both considered taking that step.

For the first time in my life, I'm thinking I'd like to have Him in my corner. Sharley and Sam don't appear to be doing too badly."

Kenan just shrugged. "Let's call it a night. I'd say the party's over. Wouldn't you?"

Chapter 7

After her return home, Sharley prayed for answers, read and reread every relevant verse in the Bible, and did everything in her power to convince herself she was better off without Kenan Montgomery. Nothing worked. Loving and trusting the Lord was the only thing that made the disappointment and heartbreak easier to bear. Sharley believed with all her heart that He wouldn't put more on her than she could endure.

She scowled at the piles of work on her desk. The lack of desire to work ranked right in there with her lack of desire to eat, sleep, and campaign. While dressing for work that morning, Sharley had assembled a mental to-do list. The list was long, work to be caught up and a campaign to be won. And she felt no excitement about any of it.

Determined to shake her lethargy, she pulled the center desk drawer open. It was packed tight with shredded bits of paper.

She tried another and found it to be the same. A tug on the last drawer handle resulted in a booby trap popping out and bouncing off her chest. She gasped and rammed her chair back into the credenza. "Devlin! Jack! Get in here!" Sharley screamed.

The two men could hardly walk for laughing.

"What's up, boss?" Devlin asked.

"You just made a couple of hours' work for yourself. That's what. I want all this paper out of here. *Now,*" she stressed angrily.

Devlin looked at Jack and back at Sharley. "It's a joke."

"Well, I'm not in the mood for your jokes. In fact, let's just discontinue the pranks as of this moment."

"Sure." Jack shrugged his shoulders, a frown touching his face. "We'll get some garbage bags and take care of the desk drawers. We didn't mean to upset you."

They quickly disappeared from the room, and Sharley felt a twinge of remorse. It wasn't their fault that the joy had gone out of her life. Her concern grew as she caught their conversation in the hallway.

"You think it was the dress?" Devlin asked.

"She's been like this ever since she came home from that party. I don't know who that woman is, but she's not our Sharley."

A grim smile touched her lips. Never had truer words been spoken. She owed them both an apology. "Devlin. Jack. Come back in here, please."

"Rats, I forgot she's got hearing like old lady Jenkins with them hearing aids on high."

Sharley smiled at that. Mrs. Jenkins was renowned for her ability to pretend she couldn't hear when she wanted to ignore people. In truth, with her hearing aids she could hear a car turn the corner half a mile from her house. They stepped into the doorway. "Guys, come in and sit down. I promise to keep the dragon lady under control."

Sharley forgave them their wary expressions as they settled before her desk. "First, I want to apologize for my bad mood. It's nothing you did. And you're right about the old Sharley. She's not here right now. Hopefully she'll be back soon, but if she never comes back, I hope you can come to love the new Sharley."

"What happened?" Devlin asked.

The sting of tears burned her eyelids, and overwhelming sadness made itself felt. "It's not something I can talk about. Let's just say God is working some changes in my life, and I need you to pray that I'll be able to accept them."

"Sure," Devlin agreed.

"If we can help, let us know," Jack added.

"Thanks, guys," Sharley said, flashing them a smile. "Right now I need you to be patient with me, and to get this paper out of my desk drawer. Where did you get it from anyway?"

"Melanie's got one of those new crosscut shredders at her office," Devlin explained. "When she told me about it, I had her bring me a bag."

"I can live with the paper, but that snake thing nearly put me in my grave," Sharley said, rising to her feet. "I'll be in the display room. Let me know when you finish. There are some papers in that center desk drawer I need this morning." She didn't mention that the papers she was eager to find were her grandmother's journal.

They took an hour to remove all the shredded bits. By the time they finished, Sharley had reprioritized her list, and all the important to-do things were going to have to wait another day. She swiveled her chair back toward the door, not quite sure why she felt the need to hide her nonwork activity as she opened the journal to the ribbon bookmark where she had left off before flying to Boston.

Just what I needed, Sharley thought, as she began to read her grandparents' love story. "I have found the man I intend to marry," Jean Reynolds wrote in her elegant flowing script. "The boy next door. Who would have believed I could love Sam so much? He is the perfect man for me. So sweet and caring."

The next few pages covered the halcyon days of her grandparents' courtship. "Sam came over today, and for the first time we were allowed to sit alone in the living room. Daddy asked me to fix lemonade, and afterward Sam seemed a little quiet. I wonder what Daddy said to him. Hopefully nothing to make him stop seeing me.

"Mary Beth taunted me today about Sam. She doesn't fool me. She thinks she can make me doubt my Sam, but it's not possible. I know he's beginning to care as deeply for me as I do for him. He's always so gentlemanly. I feel quite the lady in his company. Still, I remember the fun times we had as children and now realize that Sam looked out for me even then. I'm glad he no longer thinks of me as a little girl."

Sharley read numerous accounts of church functions attended by her grandparents. Every entry started out Sam this or Sam that, and for the first time Sharley felt the depth of her grandparents' love for each other. As Papa Sam said, probably no less than stubborn pride had been their downfall. One thought underscored her earlier doubts: Back then they had shared their faith, and yet being equally yoked had not solved their problems.

Once Papa Sam had recognized that Jean Reynolds was no longer a child, he had been persistent in his courtship. One entry had to do with his objections to her desire to bob her hair. He wanted nothing done to the glorious curly red locks. So bothersome, her grandmother lamented, but she was still pleased Sam liked her hair.

"Sam talks of going off to college, and the thought scares me so. Will he come back? Sometimes he seems so restless when he comes to visit after working all afternoon for his father. He talks constantly of the future, and I don't think he sees his future in Samuels."

"Sam came for dinner today. We had all his favorites. Daddy was his usual strict self, but Sam didn't seem troubled. Then he's probably used to it because his dad acts the same when I'm over at their house. Sam cleaned his plate and took seconds when Daddy offered.

"He winked at me when Daddy wasn't looking. That smile of his just melts my heart. I love the little dimple beside his mouth." Sharley smiled and traced a finger along her own dimple. "Sam kissed me for the first time today. I have no comparison, but surely no one could ever kiss better."

Sharley skimmed the pages of their continued courtship and then read of the wedding plans. From the description, she knew it was the event of the year in Samuels. Ben Reynolds spared no expense when it came to the marriage of his only child. There had been bridal showers and parties galore.

She read on until she reached her grandmother's entry on the first morning of her marriage: "For the first time I completely understand the importance of waiting until marriage to share our love. Our vows were the outward sign of our love, but the union was that of our body and soul. To have one without the other would have been wrong. We are one now, husband and wife forever."

Forever. Sharley reread the word. What a rude awakening life often threw into the path of unsuspecting lovers.

Already Kenan played a tremendous role in her thoughts. Sharley knew she cared more than she should. She felt a greater attraction to him than to any man she had known in the past. In truth, all others paled in significance to him.

Oh, why must there be thorns in life's garden? Perhaps to remind her of Christ's precious love. No amount of temptation had brought Jesus down from that cross, and no amount of temptation should make her regret her allegiance to her Father in heaven. Her life was His, to do with as He would, and Sharley knew He would never give her anything but the best.

Stop thinking about it, she cautioned, forcing her gaze back to the journal. "Sam is so tired of the Depression. Even though they claim we're recovering, he knows there is little likelihood his father would ever take any great risk after surviving when so many did not. Not that I would tell Sam, but I agree with Mr. Samuels. I'm sorry Sam is unhappy, but there are more important things to consider now that we have a baby on the way. Sam needs to accept that a good job and home are more important than taking chances. The one thing I want most for our unborn child is a happy home. I am most hopeful Sam will soon accept his role as businessman, husband, and father."

Her grandmother wrote of Sam's exploits: his daredevil behavior, as she called it. One way Mommy Jean seemed to deal with it was tears. Sharley frowned. Based on the recount of her tearful remonstrations to Sam Samuels, her grandmother should have owned stock in a tissue company.

Sharley shook her head. She hated manipulation. She had reacted strongly to Kenan's efforts for that very reason. Even when the manipulator was victorious, they lost because of the resentment felt by the person being controlled.

But hadn't she made the same attempt? She'd been trying to manipulate God into finding a way for her and Kenan to be together. God didn't need her input. He didn't need her to show Him what He wanted in her life. He would show her the way, and until He did, it was back to the things that were a constant in her life: God, the church, her work, her campaign, and the centennial celebration.

She had been firm with Kenan about their relationship. Now she just needed to get firm with herself and get on with her life. Sharley sighed and murmured, "The Lord's been trying to teach me patience for years. I must be a slow learner."

The phone rang, and Sharley reached for the receiver.

"I can't believe you left without talking to me," Kenan said without prelude.

"We talked. Don't you remember? It was the conversation where we decided it wouldn't work."

"Is this because I voiced my concerns to Jocelyn and not you?"

Sharley frowned. Though she didn't much care for the fact that he would admit his feelings to another woman first, that was not her concern. "No, it has more to do with the fact that you have those concerns in the first place."

"Not about you," he defended. "About the miles that separate us."

"It's more than that, and you know it. We're already hurting, Kenan. Don't make this worse on either of us."

"I'm coming to Samuels. We're going to discuss this like two rational adults."

"Stay in Boston where you belong, Kenan."

"That's just it, Sharley. I don't feel like I belong here anymore. My heart tells me I belong wherever you are. I'll be there as soon as I can catch a flight."

"Kenan, don't . . ." It was too late. He'd hung up the phone. Sharley replaced the receiver and used a tissue to dab the moisture from her eyes. He was coming. What was she going to do?

■ ■ ■ ■

"She says she's too busy. Sorry."

Kenan hesitated outside the door as Devlin went back inside. If Sharley thought she was going to avoid the situation, she had another think coming. He drew a deep breath and reached for the doorknob.

Sharley gave him the briefest of glances before she continued her task. "Visitors aren't allowed in here."

"If the mountain . . ."

"The mountain doesn't need to see Kenan Montgomery. I think we've pretty much covered everything."

Kenan noted Devlin was having difficulty with his attempts to focus his attention elsewhere. Well, if she wanted to discuss the matter in front of her employee, he would.

Before he could mutter a word, Sharley continued manipulating the face of the man on the table. Kenan tried to maintain his control, but the nausea crept over him. Sharley's gentle touch as she stroked his face and called his name woke him a few minutes later.

"I told you not to come in. It's not a corpse. Jack splashed some cleaning chemical in his eye. I was just washing it out for him."

There was a bottle of eyewash at his side, and she sounded exasperated. Kenan reached to rub the throbbing spot at the back of his head, finding he had a goose egg where he had made contact with the tiled floor. Not even the fact that his head rested in Sharley's soft lap eased the ache.

"I had to come in. This is important to me. I love you, Sharley. I don't want to lose you."

"Kenan." His name came out sounding like a sigh. "We've been through this. We're at an impasse here."

"Obviously this business means more to you than I do."

His disgruntled words only served to make Sharley push him away and get to her feet. "I won't be made to feel guilty because I have certain needs that are important to me. Montgomerys have filled important roles in this town for centuries. I won't be the first to break tradition. I'm sorry."

His movements were unsteady as he got to his feet. "And I was foolish enough to think people did all sorts of things for love."

"That's right," Sharley agreed with a steady stare. "They do."

Kenan felt almost impaled by the barbed

words. "You think I only expect you to make sacrifices? That I'm not willing to make any of my own?"

She raised her eyebrows. "I'd be giving up my business, my home, my town, my dreams, my friends, my lifestyle. What sacrifices are you willing to make? Your freedom for a ring on my finger? Pardon me if I find that a bit unequal."

Maybe she was right. It was old-fashioned to expect a woman to mold herself to the man's life. Deep down, though, Kenan knew there was more to their problem than that.

"Your fear of death is playing a bigger role in this than you realize," Sharley said softly. "You think that if I move to Boston and give up my career, we could live happily ever after."

"I don't . . ." Even as he uttered the denial, Kenan had a gut feeling she'd neatly pegged his subconscious thoughts.

"I love you, Kenan, but I have roots here. It's more than the business. I like knowing my neighbors. Hey, I even like them when they meddle in my life because I know it means they care. The need to escape is not something I share with my grandfather. In fact, I believe he could have come to love the town if he'd really given it a chance. If he'd opened his mind and become involved, he could have built a business here that would have benefited the community and kept him with his family."

She sighed. "This is what I do. It's not some little job to keep me busy until I find a husband. It's my heritage and will be my children's heritage."

"My kids aren't going to be morticians."

Sharley moved closer, almost face-to-face. "Then it's a good thing we're not getting married. Now, if you'll excuse me, I do have a body to prepare. I think you know the way out."

"Right back to impasse. Why do you insist on doing this to us both?" Kenan demanded when she turned away from him. "I'll leave, Sharley. I'll get out of your life. But fate has already dabbled in both our lives. Or maybe I should say that God has — the same God who you're always claiming to serve. I suspect we'll see each other again."

"Can't we simply be friends?"

"Friendship is a pretty pale comparison to all we could have."

"It's in God's hands, Kenan. Papa Sam reminded me that loving each other is not enough. I depend on God to light my path."

"Do you really, Sharley?" Kenan shrugged. "Maybe so. Or it could be you're so blinded by the floodlights surrounding us that you can't see the path."

Chapter 8

A few weeks later, the phone rang as she stepped into the office. Sharley rolled her eyes, positive she knew who was on the other end. The same person who tied up her fax machine all morning with his one question in giant letters: "How can we work this out if you won't talk to me?"

He was inventive, she'd give him that. She was sure the local florist loved him. The delivery truck arrived with a lead-crystal bud holder, and each day they delivered a fresh rose. Then the e-mail messages began to arrive. Sharley knew she shouldn't read them, but each one told her he hurt as badly as she did. His friends had gotten into the act, sending her references and e-mail messages, saying how miserable he was and vouching for his character. Then last night — well, the virtual flowers and cards accompanied by sentimental greetings made her want to run to Boston.

The same fax rolled out of the machine every fifteen minutes, generally followed by the ringing of the phone. Like now. She could set her clock by this man's schedule. She restrained herself from tossing the phone out the window.

She couldn't talk to Kenan right now. Her resolve wasn't strong enough. The way she felt, Sharley knew she was likely to forget all responsibilities, and she couldn't do that. Reluctantly she lifted the receiver. "Montgomery-Sloan."

"May I speak to Charlotte Montgomery?"

Relief surged through her as she realized it wasn't Kenan. She listened as a student from the high school outlined the plan to sponsor a candidate forum. "It's scheduled for the Thursday night prior to the election."

"I'll be there." She thanked him and hung up the phone.

Election day was less than three weeks away. If she hoped to find herself successful in her bid for coroner, she had to get busy. She had to make herself visible. If she marshaled her volunteer forces and made sure her personalized campaign literature was in every registered voter's hands, her chances for success would be much greater.

The fax machine went off again. "There's

no time to play, Kenan," she said determinedly. "I've got a campaign to win."

"You're doing what?"

"I'm going to Samuels. To visit Sharley."

Kenan stared at his employer, dumbfounded by the words he uttered. "Let me see if I have this right. Sam Samuels, the man who wasn't up to a trip to Samuels a few weeks ago, is going to visit his granddaughter?"

Sam nodded. "That's right. Plan to surprise her, too."

"Surprise?" Kenan sputtered. "Sam, are you sure you've given this enough thought? It's a long trip. Sure, you've got the company jet, but it's a two-hour drive from the nearest airport to Samuels."

"Cynthia's checking on a helicopter now."

Sam didn't do things in half measures. The plan was already well on its way to completion.

"What changed your mind?"

"I owe it to her."

A frown bracketed Kenan's face.

"I need to see her in her natural environment," Sam explained. "See the place where she lives, her business, meet her friends. I can't do that on the phone."

"I suppose you want me to go with you?"

Sam appeared to be deep in thought. "Not necessarily. Sharley hasn't said much, but I got the impression something happened when she was here for my party. She might not want to see you again."

The words struck dread in Kenan's heart. She probably didn't. He wondered if absence really made the heart grow fonder. He missed her — a lot, but he couldn't change that stubborn woman's mind. He might as well keep things going at home while Sam was away.

"We talked last night. She told me about Jean's journals," Sam was saying.

"There's a stack of them," Kenan said absently.

Sam's eyebrows shifted, and Kenan realized he'd given himself away. "Sharley told me a little of what she's read."

"When was that? I was under the impression that she started reading after you went to Samuels for me."

"I've visited her there. Twice."

"She told me. I've been wondering why you were so secretive."

"I didn't know how you would react to my visiting your granddaughter."

Sam shrugged. "You're a pretty decent sort of fellow. I wouldn't mind if she doesn't."

"Well, she does. Now you know. Let's leave it at that."

"Can't I at least ask what her objections to you are?"

"It's our concern." The situation between them was killing him. Kenan hadn't felt this degree of desolation in years. It was like coming home from war again, not knowing what to do, how to disconnect himself from the feelings of loss.

"Must be pretty bad for you to take on like that."

"Do you want me to accompany you to Samuels? I need to rearrange my schedule if you do."

"Marie's rescheduled your appointments for the rest of the week. Go home and pack your bag. We leave after lunch." Sam chuckled heartily at Kenan's expression, a mixture of doubt and relief.

"A surprise visit probably isn't a good idea," Kenan protested halfheartedly. "That town only has a small bed-and-breakfast."

"We'll stay with Sharley." He looked at the younger man from under his eyebrows. "I think I'm still functioning as an adequate chaperone for my granddaughter."

The trepidation Kenan felt surrendered to his joy at the thought of seeing her again.

■ ■ ■ ■

As with everything Sam Samuels did, each plan was quickly brought to completion.

"We'll be picked up at the airport and driven to Samuels. Sharley's going to be surprised."

"No doubt," Kenan mumbled, half listening to Sam as the plane sped down the runway. *In more ways than one,* he thought. His coming along was probably not the best idea, but he realized he truly did have a legitimate reason to be there. If Sam insisted on traveling to Samuels, Kenan planned to help him bear the stress of the journey. He couldn't help it if, besides the practical reason, he simply needed to see Sharley.

He hadn't felt such hopelessness in years. Sharley's refusal to respond to him hurt. A time or two he'd found himself praying for God to guide him through this troubling time. He loved her — nothing would change that. If only she would hear him out.

He'd been truthful about his doubts, but that didn't mean he believed they couldn't find solutions to the differences between them. Why was she so certain their problems were insurmountable? They didn't have to be — not if they both gave a little.

"The last time I talked with her on the phone," Sam was saying, "she was busy with the town celebration plans and was asking me what I remembered. She has so many unanswered questions. It occurs to me that it's my responsibility."

"Responsibility?"

"Sharley deserves to know about the past. Father and I often butted heads, but we loved each other. This planning committee stuff is in Sharley's blood. Her mother, grandmother, great-grandmother were all civic leaders in their time. Sharley's carrying on tradition."

"She's certainly civic-minded." Kenan noted the way Sam's gaze lingered on him, and he explained, "She took me politicking and to a church social."

Sam's grin turned into full-blown laughter.

"Don't laugh, Sam. One of your old flames gave Sharley a message for you."

"Warm regards?"

"Not exactly. Are you sure you don't want to turn around and head back to Boston?"

Sam laid his head against the seat back and stared ahead. "No, Kenan. It's time to prove you can go home again."

Kenan thought of his family, people he hadn't seen in years. Could he prove the same thing?

They arrived in Samuels just after five. In the end they had decided to drive down from the airport in a rented limo. The ride would take a little longer, but it would be smoother and more relaxing than the chopper. "Knowing Sharley, she's still at the office," Kenan said as they entered town.

But Montgomery-Sloan was locked up, and Jack was climbing in his pickup. "Kenan? Didn't think we'd see you around here again."

"I came with Sharley's grandfather."

Jack's brows lifted. "Old Sam Samuels? You're kidding?"

Kenan gestured with his head. "He's in the car. Has Sharley gone home?"

"She's over at the high school. Tonight's the meet-the-candidates forum."

Kenan frowned.

"I think Sharley would appreciate the support of her family," Jack prompted. "That's where I'm headed."

"Would you like to ride with us?" Sam called through the open window.

"Yes, sir. I'd be honored."

Jack climbed in front with the driver, and Sam lowered the dividing glass. "You say tonight's the candidate forum?"

Jack nodded. "Yes, sir. The election's next

week. This is Sharley's last chance to convince people she's right for the job."

"You believe she is?"

"I sure do. That other guy ain't qualified to wipe her shoes."

"This should be interesting."

"Mr. Samuels, sir . . ."

Kenan quickly corrected his oversight and introduced the two men. "Sam Samuels, Jack Jennings. Jack's Sharley's right-hand man."

"Call me Sam."

"Well, sir, Sharley didn't know you were coming, did she?"

"I planned to surprise her."

"You're definitely going to do that. Turn right here," he instructed the driver. "You can let us out up by the door and park in the lot. Might want to keep an eye on your car. Don't too many people see a full-fledged limo sitting around in this town. Besides the one at the funeral home, that is."

Already a crowd filled the room. Jack led the way, and Kenan followed Sam. "There she is," Jack called over his shoulder. "Sharley, look who's here."

Sharley glanced around at the sound of Jack's voice. Every drop of nervousness she had felt about the forum disappeared with the shock of seeing Kenan and Papa Sam standing there.

"Please excuse me," Sharley said to the reporter. "Papa Sam?" She leaned to kiss her grandfather's cheek. "What are you doing here?"

"We'll wait over there while you finish your interview."

"I think I have all I need," the female reporter said, her eyes moving to Kenan.

"Renee Hodson, this is my grandfather, Samuel Samuels, and a friend of the family, Kenan Montgomery."

"My pleasure. Wait, you're the Samuels who moved away, aren't you?"

"I've made my home in Boston these past years," Sam said.

The woman brightened. "I don't suppose you'd be interested in doing an interview — you know, something along the lines of local boy makes good?"

Sharley felt almost embarrassed for her. Sam's story had appeared in more publications than he could name.

"I doubt there's much about me that would interest the people of Samuels, but I thank you for asking."

"Too bad. I'd better get on over there and get a few words from Miss Montgomery's opponent. Nice meeting you both."

"So, what are you doing here?" Sharley refused to meet Kenan's eyes. She didn't need this right now. Her plate was full enough without having to deal with Kenan and their situation.

"Can't a grandfather surprise his granddaughter?"

Sharley's answer was drowned out by an overeager youth on the loudspeaker. "Ladies, gentlemen, we need to get started. Please take your seats. Can we please have all candidates on stage?"

She smiled and squeezed Papa Sam's hand. "Yes, you can surprise me."

"Go get 'em, Sharley girl," Sam whispered.

"Good luck," Kenan called, feeling inordinately happy when she stopped and smiled back at him.

The three men found seats close to the front and settled in. Kenan found himself enjoying Jack's play-by-play as the various candidates were allowed to speak. Sharley proved to be eloquent, entertaining the audience with her mixture of humor and serious repartee. Her opponent lacked her vitality, and Kenan considered him more suitable for this job of death.

Another thought occurred to him as well. The more he visited, the more he liked the town of Samuels and its inhabitants. Jack was a good person, as were the others he had met. Maybe if he gave the town more of a chance . . .

The master of ceremonies approached the microphone and announced the question-and-answer period. An old woman got to her feet. Kenan sat up even straighter when he recognized the elderly woman from the church dinner. She stood with the help of her cane, her voice carrying in the big room. "Charlotte Montgomery, will you stick around if you get this job? Now that you have Boston connections . . . Well, we know your family history."

"It's your old flame," Kenan whispered to Sam.

Sam assessed the situation. "Mary Beth Langley. Wonder what she has to do with the other candidate?"

Kenan glanced at the flyer that had been distributed. He pointed to a name. "Sharley's opponent must be her son-in-law."

He had never seen Sam move so quickly as he jumped to his feet. Kenan frowned as Sam fired back a response to Mrs. Hinson. "What I did with my personal life has no reflection on Charlotte."

"She's got your blood in her veins, Sam Samuels. Who's to say she won't up and do the same thing you did?"

"I account to no one but God above for my actions, Mary Beth, and He forgave me."

"Still cocky as ever," she mumbled. "She'll probably run off and marry that man who's been courting her."

Jack leaned over and spoke, not bothering to lower his voice. "Sharley ain't gonna have no competition if old lady Hinson don't shut up. Look how red Ray's face is. He looks like he's about to have an attack."

Kenan glanced at Sharley, noting that her cheeks were also pink. "Grandfather, Mrs. Hinson," she said, "please. The students worked hard to make this a credible event."

The voice of reason, Kenan thought as he watched the elderly adversaries settle in their seats.

"First," Sharley continued, "let me say my background speaks for itself, both professionally and personally." She stood tall, her voice clear and strong. "As for the family history, my grandfather understands that I plan to stay right here in Samuels. Some dreams are too big for small towns like Samuels. Grandfather did what he had to do. The scope of my vision is limited to this county and my life here. As for the matter of courtship, Mr. Montgomery is a friend of the family. I have no plans to marry and run away from my responsibility."

"I'd marry him in a flash," said a feminine voice, followed by a chorus of giggles.

Kenan didn't look to see where the words came from. This was turning into a fiasco.

Sharley surprised them all by laughing. "Excuse me, please. These issues have nothing to do with my qualifications for the job. I can promise you that I am dedicated to the task I've set forth for myself. Be sure to vote, and God bless you all. Thank you." She stepped away from the lectern, shook her opponent's hand, and came down the steps.

The three men rose and followed her from the gym. "Ready to run us out of town?" Sam inquired as the doors closed behind them.

"I'm sure I'll make the paper tomorrow." She fixed her eyes on her grandfather. "Was it necessary to get into a mudslinging match with Mrs. Hinson?"

"I was defending your honor. Just as you defended mine."

Sharley hesitated, surprise showing in her facial expression. "I did, didn't I? Well, she had no right making such allegations. I certainly wouldn't be running for coroner if

I planned to up and move to Boston." She slipped her hand around his arm.

Sam seemed to stand a bit taller. "Kenan and I could use a room for the night."

"You'll stay with me."

Jack held out his hand. "Give me your keys so you can ride with your grandfather. I'll drop your car by the house and walk over to pick up my truck."

"Nonsense," Sam said. "You drop her car off, and the driver can take you to pick up your vehicle. You've been very helpful, Mr. Jennings. It warms my heart to know Sharley has someone like you taking care of her."

"Call me Jack."

Kenan waited for Sam to shake Jack's hand and then stood by as he climbed into the limo, followed by Sharley.

Inside the car, she turned to him. "When did you arrive?"

"Just before the candidate's forum," Kenan answered. He glanced at Sam to make sure the elderly man was doing okay.

Sharley looked from one to the other. "It's good to see you both."

Chapter 9

Sharley threw back the cover and crawled off the bed. No sense tossing and turning the rest of the night. Sleep became an impossibility from the moment she ran into Kenan in the upstairs hallway just before bed.

"Sharley, please," he had said.

Two words and one look that spoke volumes. "Kenan, I can't talk to you," she cried out, running from him. She should have insisted he go to the bed-and-breakfast.

Sharley tiptoed down the stairs and into the kitchen, astonished at the sight of Papa Sam sitting at the kitchen table, reading his wife's journal, a cup of coffee at his elbow.

"You should be in bed."

He flashed her a shrewd look. "Old people don't need as much sleep. What's your excuse?"

"As if you didn't know." Sharley filled a cup with coffee and sat down. She cupped it in both hands and took a sip.

Her grandfather smiled. "I asked Kenan what your objections to him were. He said they were personal."

"They are."

"And history repeats itself."

Sharley's finger ceased tracing the cup rim, and her head flew up. "I'm sorry. I love him, but I can't be with him."

"These journals are a pretty true representation of our lives. I've learned all sorts of things about Jean that I didn't know. A man should be smart enough to know his pregnant wife was feeling insecure. I can't believe she ever thought I'd fall out of love with her. As for Mary Beth Langley, well, Mary Beth was the one to be pitied. I tried to take care of Jean. As far as I was concerned, she had never been prettier. Why would she think I was unhappy?"

"Weren't you?"

Sam laid the journal on the table. "Not with her. But I felt trapped. We were kids. I was barely eighteen when Glory was born. Jean had her doubts, too. What was it she said?" Sam thumbed back in the journal and read, " 'Not so young but not so old considering the monumental step of bringing a child into the world.' So true. She was so sure a boy would make me happy."

"I was surprised to learn Great-Grandfather Reynolds died the night before Mother was born. Mommy Jean was sure the baby would lift his spirits."

"Her grief brought on the labor. I prayed nothing would happen to either of them. She's right about Glory being a beautiful baby. All pink and rosy, with my dark hair and Jean's green eyes." The love was there in his eyes for anyone who looked to see.

"Were you upset because she named Mom Gloria?"

"I hated that name," Sam said. "Still do. I thought Charlotte was a much prettier name. I had no idea she made a vow to her father to name the child after her mother. I wouldn't have objected if I'd known."

"She says you were a good father," Sharley pointed out. "I liked the parts where she described how Mother was all smiles when she was with you."

"I did love your mother, Sharley. My wife and daughter were the only bright spots in my life. I'd go to work, and Father refused to allow any newfangled ideas in his business. I resented him, and the discontent spilled over into my personal life as well. My mother died, and I was devastated. I loved her so much. Father became even more rigid. Mother had a way of convincing him to at least think about things."

"What about the hardware store?"

"Jean was busy at home, and I was at the bank, so I hired a manager. When Glory grew older, Jean started taking over. The business did well, and she was so excited about her success."

"Why didn't you help her?" Sharley asked.

"Jean was an old-fashioned wife. If I had shown an interest in the hardware business, she would have turned over the reins to me. I couldn't take that away from her. I never knew exactly how bad I hurt her," Papa Sam said brokenly. "Listen to this. 'Sam left me today,' " he read. " 'He will always be the love of my life, but I'm not ready to traipse around the world and drag our daughter away from the only home she has ever known. I've lived that life, and it is not what I want for my child. For the first time in my life, I feel I am where I should be, and my only wish is that Sam shared that sentiment.' "

The heartbreak in Mommy Jean's written words brought tears to Sharley's eyes. She nodded slowly. "There are other journals where she describes her childhood, how she missed her mother, how hard her father was on her. She found contentment in Samuels. It was her first settled home."

"One parent for her child in a secure setting, or two in an unsettled environment. What a choice," Sam said with a shake of his head. "I remember the day like it was yesterday. Jean described me as distraught. No doubt I was. I wanted to make a loan to an inventor, and my father called me an idiot and ordered me to stop this foolishness. He embarrassed me in front of everyone. I walked out, came home, and ordered Jean to pack our bags. Glory was six, and Jean kept on and on about our wonderful life here in Samuels and Glory's school and friends. She insisted we could work it out. That night, after Jean went to bed, the scene kept playing in my head. I got angry. If she didn't trust me to provide for her and our child, I decided she should stay in Samuels with my father. I wrote her a note and ran like a thief in the night."

He shook his head. "She was right about my pride. Father was sure I would come back, but I was determined to prove him wrong. Like she said, I would have lived on the streets before asking my father for a job."

"But why did you let it go for so long? How could the two of you not communicate when you obviously loved each other?"

"Like you and Kenan?"

"Yes," Sharley snapped. She sighed. "It's

different. He's not my husband. And even if things were different, I couldn't marry him. He doesn't have the same commitment to God that I have, after all. In the meantime, I can't talk to him — he tempts me too much."

Sam patted her arm. "Makes you want to throw off the ties and take off for Boston, does he?"

"Not particularly Boston. Just wherever he is."

"Now we're getting somewhere."

Sharley hated his happy grin. "No, we aren't. There's too much at stake. I'm committed to God, yes, but I'm also committed to my life here."

"Try telling your heart that. And make sure you're really listening to God and not putting words in His mouth."

She settled the cup back onto the table. "I have done nothing but pray about this, Papa Sam. I just go around in circles."

"I have good feelings about the two of you."

"You do? Why? I thought you were bothered because he's not a Christian."

"Maybe not yet, but the Lord is using you to work miracles in Kenan's life. I just know it."

"I don't," Sharley said, feeling even more

skeptical than before.

He smiled at her sadly. "Even if I wanted to, I can't go back and change my life, Sharley. I distanced myself from everyone who loved me because I thought it was what I had to do. I didn't ask Jean how she felt, and now all these years later, I read how I hurt her. I didn't ask God what He intended either. Obviously part of my plans were good. I've been successful in business, able to help a great number of people get their start — but at what cost to myself? Maybe if I had waited on the Lord, instead of rushing off under my own steam, eventually He would have worked out all our lives so that we could all have been happy. Instead, I nearly lost everything that was important to me."

"Nearly?"

"You haven't finished reading this journal, have you?"

Sharley shook her head.

"Can I ask why you left me this one to read?"

She hesitated, searching for the truth. "So you could see what your leaving did to Mommy Jean and Mother," she said at last.

"I thought so," Sam said softly. "Thank you for the truth. What you haven't read yet will probably shock you. Jean and I shared some wonderful times after I left."

His words confused Sharley. "I don't understand."

"A year passed, and Jean came to see me. She refused to accept that our love had died. She was like a child, guilty one moment, excited the next, but we spent two weeks together. She told her family she was in New York." Sam chuckled heartily. "She made me take her clothes shopping before she left."

No one had ever known that Mommy Jean had visited Boston with Papa Sam. Sharley stared at her grandfather.

"Those visits rejuvenated us both," Sam said. "She took about four long vacations a year. Not just to Boston. We traveled extensively. It wasn't a normal marriage — but it was still a marriage."

"So you didn't need pictures to know how Mommy Jean and Mother looked. I'm sure she kept you current."

"Until her death."

"So you knew about me?"

He nodded. "I knew when your mother married, and I knew she had a baby girl. I had no idea what happened to you after your grandmother's death."

"And you were never tempted to find out?"

"I did find out. When Kenan came to Samuels."

"I don't know what to say," Sharley said. "I told myself I didn't hold it against you, but obviously I did."

"I can only ask you to pray about the situation, Sharley. To try and find it in your heart to forgive an old man who made a bunch of mistakes."

Both of them looked up as Kenan stepped into the kitchen. "What are you two doing up so early?"

They stared at each other. Only then did they realize they had talked the night away.

Chapter 10

Sam and Kenan left on Monday morning, and Sharley found herself tearful as she hugged Sam. "I'm glad you came."

"Me, too, Sharley girl."

"Now that my eyes have been opened, I know that God can use everything that's happened to us. The Bible says that all things work together for good for those who are called according to His purposes, and I see that now. And I thank God for bringing you back to me."

Tears misted the old eyes. "I love you."

She hugged him close. "I love you, too. We're going to spend more time together. I promise."

"I look forward to it."

Sam climbed into the back of the car, and Kenan stood, waiting and watching. "Good-bye, Kenan," Sharley said softly. "It was good seeing you."

"I'm glad you and Sam were able to work

things out. Do you think we'll ever be able to do the same?"

"I honestly don't know, Kenan," she admitted. Tears trailed along her cheeks as she forced a watery smile. "I haven't been fair to you, but truth is, I'm afraid of what I'd say or do if we talked. I love you, but I can't go to Boston. In the interest of fairness, I can't ask you to give up your life there to come here."

"What if I said I would?"

"I'd say give yourself some time to think about it. Pray about it. Don't make a decision you'll come to regret later in life. I refuse to be the Sam and Jean of our generation."

"Can I kiss you good-bye?"

She stepped forward and lost herself in his tender embrace. Neither wanted to let go. Sharley felt regret for the lost weekend, time she could have shared with him.

"If I call, will you talk to me?"

"Not until I get everything straight in my head. You'd better go. I think Papa Sam's eager to get home."

"Good luck with the election. I think you'll make a fine coroner."

She pushed back her surprise and squeezed his hand. "I'll do my best. Good-bye." After she broke away, she stood and waved as they drove away.

In her office, Sharley sat and thought about the visit. They had visited the old home place, Papa Sam saying he understood why she preferred her house to that one. He teased her about nothing in the town being any different than he remembered from his youth. On Sunday morning, he and Kenan accompanied her to church. In the classroom, Sharley got her first glimpse of the type of father Papa Sam would have been, the great-grandfather he still could be, as he entertained the small children with Bible stories.

Pastor George's sermon stomped on their toes as he preached on forgiving and forgetting. One verse opened her eyes, 1 John 4:20, "If anyone says, 'I love God,' yet hates his brother, he is a liar. For anyone who does not love his brother, whom he has seen, cannot love God, whom he has not seen."

Hate seemed a strong word, but Sharley knew she had lied to herself for so many years, pretending her grandfather's abandonment didn't matter. Her method of dealing with it had been to ignore, not forget and forgive. Sharley asked Sam to join her at the altar, and together they prayed that God would touch their hearts and help them to share the rest of their lives in a spirit of love and family.

Now Jack stepped into the office. "Hi, Sharley. Mr. Sam get off okay?" At her nod, he asked, "How did it go? You two enjoy your visit?"

"You were right, Jack. Family is important. Once you get beyond the petty stuff, you realize that even more."

"Mr. Sam seems to be a good man, but then I already knew that. I've had the pleasure of knowing his daughter and granddaughter, and they do any man proud."

"Thanks, Jack."

The rest of the week was hectic. Sharley was still intent on her campaigning, spending days and evenings contacting the county residents.

One morning before work she found the time to finish reading the journal and felt even more amazed that her grandparents had carried on a secret relationship for so many years. She didn't pretend to understand why they chose to keep it secret. Sharley doubted Sam could tell her the reason. In her heart, she felt certain the two of them had been in love but unsure how to handle the situation. Together they had let it go on until too late. Because Mommy

Jean never confided the truth to her daughter, her mother had never bonded with her father.

Sharley shook her head at the thought. *Such a loss. In life, no one is more important than family.* Even as she thought the words, Sharley felt a sense of something gone wrong, but the feeling soon passed.

The phone rang, and she reluctantly marked her place and closed the journal before lifting the cordless to her ear. "Sorry to bother you, Sharley, but the Timmonses and Williamsons are here to make arrangements."

"John and Leslie? Jim and Allison? What arrangements?"

"Their boys. You didn't hear?"

"Hear what?" She hadn't read the paper or turned on the television for days.

"The boys went joyriding last night. There was an accident involving drinking and a high-speed chase. Jeff and Lynn were killed."

Sharley found herself at a total loss for words. "I'll be right there."

As she dressed, she prayed God would give her the right words of reassurance for these parents deprived of their loved ones by such senseless acts of utter stupidity.

She arrived at her office to find two teary

mothers and two fathers who were intent on being strong for their wives. They went through the process on automatic, making decisions none of them had ever expected to make in their lifetimes. Both boys were football stars, and the high school had offered the use of the auditorium. The joint funerals were scheduled for Wednesday at one in the afternoon.

Sharley hugged Allison and then Leslie, and said, "I'm so sorry. If we can be of service to you in any way, please let me know."

Leslie Timmons dug in her purse and pulled out a photo. "This was my beautiful boy," she sobbed as she placed it in Sharley's hand. "Please give him back to me for the funeral." Tears streamed down her face. "I don't think I could stand it if he didn't look like himself."

The grief-filled words presented a daunting challenge. From what Devlin had told her when she arrived, Sharley knew this young man had been thrown from the vehicle upon impact. She breathed a prayer and nodded. "I'll do everything possible."

The woman gave a feeble smile and said, "You'll do a good job. You always do."

"My husband is going to talk to the coach about his team members serving as pallbearers," Allison said softly. "We'll drop off his letter jacket later today."

After they left, Sharley went into the back and started her job. Tears streamed down Sharley's face as she worked. The waste of such young lives tore at her heart. Temptation stronger than they could defeat had been their downfall.

"You okay, Sharley?" Jack asked.

"No. I need a few minutes to pull myself together."

"Go ahead. I'll take care of this."

In the employee bathroom, Sharley allowed the tears to fall freely. "They're in Your hands, God. Keep them and be with those they left behind."

Left behind. How apt a description for those left to face the loss. Sharley wondered how big a part her own desolation played in her grief for these two children. She felt abandoned, left behind because she couldn't be the woman Kenan wanted her to be and he couldn't be the man she needed him to be.

CHAPTER 11

"What's wrong with you? You've been moping around this office for days." Kenan looked up at his boss, wondering why Marie hadn't warned him of Sam's arrival. Probably because she hadn't had time. Sam had a way of popping up when he was least expected. And right now Kenan wasn't too sure he wanted to answer any questions. He wasn't sure he could for that matter.

"I'm not moping."

"Hmmph." Sam rolled his eyes and settled into a chair before the desk. "You might as well get it off your chest."

Kenan glared at him. "Your granddaughter is a royal pain."

"Tell me something I don't already know. I talked with her yesterday. I'd say she's suffering from the same malady as you."

"She's miserable, too?" He leaned forward, eager to hear what Sam had to say.

"Not that she'd admit it, but it sure

sounded that way to me."

"This mess is all your fault," Kenan complained. "If you hadn't sent me to handle your business, I'd never have met up with Sharley Montgomery and my life would have been a lot simpler."

"Oh, you'd have met her sooner or later. I think God had a plan all along for you to meet."

Kenan thought about that for a moment, then shrugged. "I don't know what else I can do. She's made up her mind and says it's in God's hands. What kind of answer is that?"

"A Christian's life is always in the Father's hands, Kenan. If you can't understand that much, you don't deserve Sharley."

"Oh, I understand, and I'm not saying there's anything wrong with her beliefs. I just don't understand this stuff about harnesses or whatever it is. Did I tell you her pastor cornered me at the dessert table at the church social? I think he was trying to feel me out."

Sam guffawed with laughter. "It's yokes, Kenan, not harnesses. Tell me, how would you deal with Charlotte's religion if you were her husband?"

"Things haven't advanced that far," Kenan protested uncomfortably.

"Do you love her? Are you considering you might like to have her in your life?" At Kenan's reluctant nod, he added, "Then you're contemplating marriage. And I won't have you playing fast and loose with my granddaughter."

"This is between Sharley and me, Sam," Kenan said, a hint of warning in his voice. "We discussed your role in the matter when I first traveled to Samuels, and Sharley says you have nothing to do with our decisions. I have to agree."

"I have the right of an old man who loves both of you."

"I'll concede to that." Kenan rubbed his eyes. They were on fire from lack of sleep. Every night he went to bed, hoping he'd exhausted himself with a strenuous workout, and every night he spent half the night thinking about the situation with Sharley and wondering what he could do to make things right. "I would accept her religion," he admitted with a sigh. "In fact, whatever happens between her and me, I think I already have accepted her religion."

The old man gave him a keen-eyed glance. "What do you mean by that?"

"I —" Kenan hesitated. "Well, there's nothing wrong with going to church. If she and I were together, I'd go to church with her and see to it that our children were in church as well."

"You wouldn't send them like your mother sent you?"

He shook his head. "I wouldn't expect them to have a faith I didn't share. Maybe that's why my belief in Christ never amounted to much, because I was too influenced by my parents' example. I did go to church as a child and even some as a teen, but they never went with me. I sort of dropped out of church after I got back from Nam. Christ didn't seem very real to me."

"You stopped seeking the Lord when you needed Him the most," Sam pronounced sadly. "He could have provided you with answers if you'd been willing to open your heart and listen."

"I did listen, and I didn't like the answers I was getting. It was all so senseless. I hated that part of my life. I only wanted to be left alone."

"I don't believe you did. I think you wanted to understand the senseless killing. And you felt a little guilty that you didn't die with the others."

Kenan had a sinking feeling Sam was right on target. He had certainly been unable to settle in any one place for a number of years. Then the nightmares had begun to recede slightly, and he was able to get on with his life. But an emotional wound had been left behind, always there no matter how well he hid it.

"What does it matter?" He sighed. "Even if we could work out the religion thing, I'd have to move to Samuels. Heaven only knows what's there for me in terms of work."

"I hope you're planning to give me sufficient notice?" The old man gave him a roguish grin.

"For what?" Exasperated, Kenan rolled his eyes. "That stubborn Sharley won't give me the time of day. She wants to be friends. Friends," he spat. "What man wants to be friends with the woman he loves?"

"Oh, I don't know. Seems to me not so long ago you were offering Jocelyn marriage based on friendship. At least she had the good sense to refuse you. Let me tell you something you don't know, Kenan. There are two things you'll find in any great marriage — one is God in the home, and the other is friendship. Love grows from friendship. Many a man and woman have married their best friend."

"So you think I should be Sharley's friend?"

"I think you should get your life in order.

You have to get right with Jesus Christ. And then you have to decide if you're willing to give up Boston. If you can't, don't tease her with the possibility of a future. It's not fair to either of you."

Kenan lifted his shoulders. "No. You probably noticed how she wouldn't give me the time of day when we were in Samuels. I haven't felt so desolate since I was in Nam. I don't know what to do."

"Have you considered prayer? For the right reasons, I mean? Not because you want to be with Sharley but because you believe God died for your sins and because you want to know His master plan for you?"

"I have been praying, Sam." He looked embarrassed, and the gray eyebrows across the desk shifted a degree higher. "I've been praying pretty much along the lines you just said. Whatever happens with Sharley, I know now that I need God in my life. I need Him to be more than an idea that I think about now and then. I want the kind of living relationship with Him that I see in you and Sharley." He shoved his fingers through his hair. "Oh, I know neither one of you is perfect, and you both make mistakes. But you have something with God that I now know I need." He sighed. "I guess I might as well confess what I've been thinking lately. I am a Christian, Sam."

Sam's eyebrows shot higher than Kenan had ever seen them. "Why didn't you tell Sharley? Me?"

"Because I guess I've been embarrassed. I'm not sure I can ever be the Christian either of you are. I feel as though I don't deserve to claim my salvation."

"Few of us do," Sam pointed out. "But you believe. That's a first step."

Kenan could sense the man's excitement. "I'd have told you before if I knew it meant that much to you."

"I've been after you for years. I can't believe you didn't say anything before."

Kenan shrugged. "I've turned my back on God for so long I'm not even sure He's willing to let me back into the flock."

"Remember the parable of the good shepherd? To Christ you are more precious than anything else. You know, I think I'll rest easier tonight now that you've shared this." He leaned forward and met Kenan's eyes. "Get your life straight, Kenan. When I go to heaven, I want to do so knowing I'll see you again."

Kenan smiled at that. "I'd hate to think I'd never see you again either," he whispered after Sam had gone.

Sam's words played around in Kenan's

head, pulling his concentration away from the piles of work on his desktop. Finally he gave up and began to pray.

Sharley had remained firm in her resolve to keep her distance from him. What an effective witness she was. So many people would put their own needs and desires before service to God. Not his Sharley. She was right. Their relationship was in the Lord's hands. Just as it should be.

Repent. Well, he'd already done that. Now he bowed his head, and at last he felt the acceptance of Jesus' loving arms. Then he reached for the phone. He wanted to make an appointment with the pastor to discuss this new commitment to God that he'd made.

Before he could place the call, the door was flung open and a hysterical Marie cried, "It's Sam. He's in trouble."

He sprang to his feet and raced across the hallway. "Sam?"

The man was obviously in agony. Kenan began loosening Sam's tie. "Sam, what's happening? Is it your heart? Where's your medicine?"

Kenan patted Sam's pockets in search of his nitro. How many times had he warned him? "Call 911. Get his nitroglycerin. In the desk drawer." Kenan had never seen

Sam's efficient secretary so flustered. She seemed incapable of movement. "Now!" he yelled.

Sam's grasp on his arm was feeble as he said. "It's too late, Kenan," he gasped. "Remember what I said. I love you, son. Tell Sharley I love her too. And tell her what you just told me."

"Sam. Noo!"

"Sharley?" Devlin called her name softly as he tapped on the door. "You have a call. I tried to take a message, but he says it's extremely urgent."

She grabbed a fresh tissue and dabbed at her eyes. It was probably one of the boys' fathers calling with another request. "Tell him I'll be right there." She went to her office and picked up the phone.

"Sharley?"

"Kenan," she groaned upon recognizing his voice. "I can't do this right now."

"Sharley, are you okay? Have you been crying?"

"No, I'm not okay. My life is miserable, and I think we both know why."

"And I'm about to add to that," he muttered.

"What? If you have something to say, just say it."

Still he hesitated, and Sharley felt tempted to thrust the receiver back into the cradle and run until she couldn't run anymore. Quickly she offered up a prayer for strength.

"Sharley," he said at last, his voice gentle, "Sam died about thirty minutes ago."

She froze. Sam couldn't be dead. She hadn't had a chance to visit him again — to share her life with him. "No," she gasped.

"Sharley?" The frightened tone of his voice told her how much he cared for her. "Sharley, honey, are you okay? Say something. Please."

"How?" The question was the only word she could croak past the growing lump in her throat.

"Heart attack. He had just left my office. Sam was gone before the ambulance arrived. I was with him when he died."

She felt herself wavering on her emotional tightrope. "I'm glad he wasn't alone." Silence stretched between them. The tears returned, chasing each other down her cheeks.

"If I'd just been able to get him his medicine sooner," Kenan murmured.

His distress was so obvious, his words choked. The need to comfort him overwhelmed Sharley. She knew he loved Sam, and his connection to the old man was stronger than hers. "Don't blame yourself. You did all you could."

"He had just finished telling me he wanted to see me again in heaven."

Sharley managed a teary smile. "So do I."

"You will."

Had she imagined the words? "Kenan, are you okay?"

"What can I do to help?" he asked, ignoring her question. "Would you like for me to arrange for extra cars for the procession?"

"I'm sorry. What?"

"Extra cars. There's going to be a number of people flying in for the funeral. They'll need transportation from the airport."

"Of course," she said, recalling the job she had to do. "What about services? Papa Sam requested a memorial service in Boston. He gave me a list of the people he wanted at the graveside services here."

"It's all being kept very private. The office is not releasing any information to the press."

"I'll caution my guys to keep it quiet as well. And I'll arrange for limos to pick everyone up at the airport."

"Sharley, will you come to Boston for the memorial service?"

"When is it?"

"Thursday morning."

"I've got two funerals on Wednesday. I'll get a flight out just as soon as possible."

"I can send the company jet."

Sharley almost refused and then realized she didn't want to. "That'll be fine. I'll let your secretary know the exact time just as soon as everything is finalized."

"There's the matter of the business. I'm going to have my hands full."

"The suddenness must have . . ." Sharley felt choked by the words.

"Sam had set certain safeguards in place to assure nothing interfered with business."

They both fell silent, as grief washed over them in a deep tide. Then Sharley said, "I'm going to bury him beside Mommy Jean. I'll have a new grave marker cut."

"Nice thing to do for old Triple S."

A weak smile touched her lips. "Did he tell you that he and Mommy Jean saw each other regularly after he left Samuels?"

"You're kidding."

"According to her journals, they stayed in touch by letter and then got together several times a year for vacations. She loved him, you know. I hope he knew I loved him, too."

"He does. The last thing he said was to tell you he loved you. I like to think he's reunited in heaven with your grandmother and mom and all the people from Samuels."

"You think maybe they finally found a place where they can live happily ever after?" she asked, a wistfulness filling her voice.

"I'm sure of it. Sharley, will you call me if you need me?"

The silence stretched over the distance, and she knew that he waited for an answer. Now was a time for leaning if ever there was one, and God would want her to share her grief with this man Sam had loved.

"I need you now," she admitted. "Talk to me, Kenan."

"Sharley, honey, I'm so sorry. I don't know what to say."

"You don't have to say anything in particular. I know you loved Sam and he loved you. I talked to him yesterday, and he voiced his concern about our unhappiness."

The conversation stretched on and on, neither wanting to say good-bye. There was consolation in sharing.

"I've got to go," Sharley said finally. "There's a lot to be done before I can get there on Thursday. I'll contact a funeral home there in Boston to handle the embalming for me. If you don't mind, how about contacting his pastor and making arrangements for the memorial service? Did he leave any last-minute requests?"

"Nothing other than he be buried in Samuels in the family plot."

Tears flooded down her face. "Oh, Kenan, he wanted to come home."

Chapter 12

Kenan found himself watching everything Sharley did and feeling impressed and proud of the way she carried out every detail of Sam's burial. Now, though, the graveside service was over, and her professionalism was beginning to crack around the edges. His heart broke as he watched her dabbing her eyes with a handkerchief. If only she would allow him to hold her, to comfort her.

"I'm sorry, Sharley."

"Me, too." She sniffed and turned to make her way to the family car.

"Sharley, please," Kenan said, catching her arm. "I know I said a lot of things the last time we were together. But so much has changed. I've missed you."

"I know, Kenan. Can we discuss this later?"

"Okay, so I was stubborn."

"You were waiting for me to throw in the

towel and come running to you. I thought about it a time or two, but nothing has changed. I still have my business, and I'm still running for coroner."

"Good. How's the election looking?" The uncertainty in her expression proved he had garnered her attention.

"Pretty good, I think."

"I'm sure you'll be victorious. I'm sorry this had to happen right now. I know it's not a good time."

"There's never a good time to lose someone you love, is there, Kenan?"

"No. Sharley, I have to fly Sam's friends back to Boston. We'll be leaving in an hour."

She nodded. "I'm serving refreshments at the house if you'd care to stop by. I've invited the others already."

"That was nice of you."

She shrugged. "I figured somebody should do something. He was my grandfather. I'll miss him."

"I'm sorry the two of you didn't get an opportunity to meet earlier," Kenan said.

"Me, too."

"Sounds as though you've forgiven him."

She nodded and blinked away her tears. "I'm so glad God gave us the chance to work things through the last time I saw him."

"You know he left a will. His attorney wants a few words with us."

She sighed. "I hope you're his beneficiary. I've got just about everything I need right here."

"Everything?" Kenan asked softly. *Tell me,* his heart cried. *Tell me I mean as much to you as you do to me.*

She looked away. "I've got to finish things here and get over to the house, Kenan."

She had invited the entire town, Kenan realized as he recognized a few faces from his time spent in Samuels. He was amazed that they remembered him, and all took time to thank him for being there in Sharley's time of need.

"Good to see you again, Kenan," Pastor George said as he took the seat beside him.

"You, too, Pastor."

"Sharley seems to be holding up well."

Kenan glanced at him. "I'm afraid she's more upset than she's letting on. She won't let me help."

"What happened between the two of you?"

The need to confide in the man was suddenly overwhelming. "Is there somewhere private we can talk?"

"I'm sure Sharley wouldn't mind if we went out on the patio."

Kenan found that once he opened up, the

words poured freely. He told Pastor George about his time in Vietnam and about his recent commitment to Christ. The man said very little, only nodded his head now and then.

"Would you like me to pray with you, Kenan?"

"I'd be honored, Pastor George."

"I have one other question I need answered first. Are you making your commitment to Jesus because of Sharley and Sam?"

Kenan knew there was only one honest answer. "Probably, but not for the reason you think. I love them both, and I do want to be with them in heaven — but because of what I saw in their lives, I finally understand I need God in my own life, now more than ever. I've been lost for a long time. There are longings inside me that places and people can't fill. When I was a child we sang of the friend we have in Jesus. I want that friendship now. More than ever."

Pastor George grasped Kenan's hand in his. "Then let's pray."

All the burdens seemed to lift up and drift away as Kenan listened to the man's words.

Sharley wondered where Kenan had gotten to. Papa Sam's attorney had approached her a few minutes before and requested a private meeting before they left for Boston. She told him she would find Kenan.

She stepped out onto the patio and hesitated. Kenan and Pastor George were in prayer. Hopes that had been dashed suddenly seemed to skyrocket joyously. Sharley forced them back for fear that she was wrong.

Pastor George was the first to spot her and glanced at Kenan. Kenan nodded his head, and the pastor summoned her into their little group.

"I thought you might like to know Kenan has recently made a commitment to God."

She flung her arms about Kenan's neck, happy that he enfolded her in his tender arms and held her near. "Oh, Kenan, this is so wonderful."

Neither of them were aware when Pastor George quietly went inside the house. "You might want to give them a few minutes," he told Sam's lawyer when the man came to stand in the doorway.

The lawyer pulled two letters from inside his coat. "I'll just give them these, and we can talk later."

Sharley and Kenan looked up at the man. "I'm sorry to disturb you, but Sam asked that you read these carefully and consider what he has to say."

"Thank you, Mr. Glenn. We'll be in to see you shortly. Read your letter, Kenan. Let's see what Papa Sam has to say."

They settled into the glider, each intent on this last communication from the man they had loved.

Kenan,

You're the son I never had. It's been a true pleasure teaching you the ropes and watching you grow from the shell of a man who first came into my company. Now, only because I don't want that shell to return, I make this suggestion to you. Open a second branch of the business in Samuels. You've been at odds with the situation between you and Sharley for a while now, and the time has come to pursue your happiness. If you can't get the girl out of Samuels, turn the town into a place where you'd want to live and stay there with her. She's worth the battle. It's about time I did something decent for the town and my family. I'd like to think I could do that through you — but most importantly of all, I want you to do something for yourself. God can give you the peace you need, if you will only open your heart and let Him in. I'm hoping to see you again in heaven.

Kenan blinked furiously and reached for Sharley's hand. She squeezed it and picked up her own letter.

Well, Sharley, it's happened. A force much greater than the two of us has separated us again. Like you, death carries no worries for me. As the years passed and the body weakened, so has my desire to remain on this earth. I've looked forward to my heavenly journey for so long. You have been a bright shining star in these last days, and I can say I've been wonderfully rewarded to leave someone like you behind to carry on. You made me realize what I gave up by leaving Glory behind, and though I know I have God's forgiveness in the matter, I pray that one day you, too, can forgive an old man for his stubborn pride.

Tears streamed unchecked down her face for several minutes, and Kenan placed an arm about her shoulder to comfort her. She wiped her eyes and picked up the letter again.

I know Samuels is the home of your

heart, and I will not ask you to relocate to Boston. The business there pretty much runs itself these days, but if you prefer, you may sell your inheritance and invest the proceeds in Samuels. I'm leaving this to your discretion. Kenan and I have discussed your concerns for the town, and hopefully it's not too late to revitalize and renew.

As for Kenan, I don't know if the two of you can leap beyond the differences, but the world will be richer for your love if you do. You've helped him remember that while death may be an ending here on earth, it's a beginning in heaven. Whatever you decide, live in joy and peace and know that you've always been much loved by the one you called Papa Sam.

Sharley dropped the pages into her lap. "Oh, Kenan." She turned to face him, amazement in her eyes.

He smiled. "I've got a long way to go before I'll be the man I want to be for you, but now that Sam's prodding," he said, waving the letter, "has boosted my courage, I want to ask if you would consider marrying me one day. You don't have to answer now."

Her eyes shone. "Yes, I do. The Lord has

opened my eyes to a lot of things here today. He's shown me that you are indeed the man He chose for me, and He's taught me about forgiveness, particularly for those you love. Papa Sam may never know how much I love him, but it's my intention to make you very aware of how much you're loved. And Kenan, there's something else. I won't insist that we live in Samuels. I may have to travel back and forth frequently, but I'll go to Boston with you."

Kenan hugged her close. "Oh, Sharley darling, thank you for loving me. I've never been so miserable as I was when you sent me away."

She smiled at him. "But you didn't give up. The faxes and the e-mail references were pretty good."

"Liked those, did you?"

"I'm sorry I led you on and then ran away when things weren't going exactly like I thought they should. I should have trusted God to make them right."

He brushed her face with his fingers. "I won't ask you to leave Samuels. There's nothing in Boston for me, now that I've learned belonging with someone takes precedence over a lot of things."

"Belonging?"

"Wanting to be in a place because all the

ties in the world make it the most important place in the world for you to be."

Sharley nodded. "Oh, Kenan, I can't wait to marry you. And you know what the best thing of all is?"

"Um, what?" Kenan asked after kissing her.

"We won't have to argue over whether I take your name. I'll already have it."

"But you would agree to take it formally?"

"I won't go through the rest of my life as Charlotte Montgomery Montgomery, if that's what you mean. As far as the world is concerned, I'll be your wife and the mother of the children who also bear your name. But you allowing me to be myself, well, that's the most precious gift you're giving me. Are you sure you'll be able to give up the big city for this?"

"All the excitement in the world doesn't compare to the joy of being here with you. Besides, Boston wouldn't be the same without Sam."

They fell silent for a few moments as both considered their loss. Sharley's time with the elderly man she had come to love had been too short. Kenan owed him his life, for it had been Sam who helped him fight off the nightmare of Vietnam. And it had been Sam who had led him to find the true love of his life.

"I think maybe he knew his days were numbered," Kenan mused. "Sam kept asking when I was going to get my head screwed on right. Said he wanted to see me again in heaven and that you were too much of a woman to lose because of some old fears. I was holding his hand when he died. And you know, for the first time, death didn't seem like such a frightening, terrible thing."

She met his eyes. "I know how much my business has freaked you out. Are you really going to be able to handle that?"

He nodded, his gaze filled with love. "Even knowing you'll always have the business doesn't make me want to run the other way."

"And if you get caught in the backlash of some of our jokes?"

He grinned. "I'll have a few of my own."

Sharley smiled as Kenan wrapped her in his loving embrace. Their lips met, sealing the commitment of forever. Not even the darkness of her career could dim their bright future.

EPILOGUE

"Happy anniversary, my love."

Sharley twisted in the hammock and looked at her husband's face. "Nineteen years. Who would have thought it?"

"God," Kenan supplied with a broad grin. "He certainly knew me better than I knew myself. He knew I needed you to lead me back to Him. I'm so glad you came into my life."

The intervening years had been good to them. God had seen fit to make them the parents of two beautiful children — one not-so-somber daughter and a son who had inherited his father's love of flying.

"So how do you feel about Samantha's career choice?"

Kenan knew she was thinking of the vow he'd uttered so many years ago, before he understood he needed her in his life; he would never have suspected that one day he might accept the fact that his daughter wanted to be a funeral director. He smiled. "I think if it's what she wants, it's what she should do."

Sharley grimaced in good humor. "That certainly ranks up there with every evasive answer you've ever given me."

He laughed. "Sharley darling, you know I was never certain I wanted my children to take over your business."

"But dealing with me and my business has become easier over the years, hasn't it?"

"You've made it easy," Kenan said. The hammock rocked with the breezes of late spring that stirred the sweet scent of flowers about them. "You've even made death come alive for me." Sharley looked puzzled by his strange comment. "Your love has shown me that morticians are people to be admired. Your caring has helped relieve the suffering of so many people over the years. I've seen the faces of the bereaved, and now I understand their pleasure at doing this one last right thing for their loved ones. You've helped me understand that death is just a part of life. In fact, I see now that it's the door that leads from this life into a fuller, richer life. And when the day comes that God sees fit to separate us, I'll know my life has been enriched by having you in it. Our children will carry on what we are and for that I'm eternally grateful."

"Mom? Dad?"

Kenan called an answer to their daughter. He looked at her with pride as she crossed the lawn. She was the young version of Sharley all over again, beautiful, full of life.

Sammy was waving a letter. "It came. I've been accepted."

Sharley almost tumbled them out of the hammock as she sat up. She glanced back at Kenan, and he winked, his lined face curving into a deep smile.

"Oh no, not another gravedigger," he teased.

"Ah, Daddy," Sammy groaned, and their laughter filled the air.

Dear Reader,

I love calling North Carolina home. For me, *A Sense of Belonging, Carolina Pride,* and *Look to the Heart* reflect the heart and soul of North Carolina — home and family.

Always an avid reader, I dreamed of becoming a librarian, but circumstances prevailed and I work full time in an office.

After losing my parents in 1991 and having my own medical crises in 1992, I accepted I couldn't do it alone. I gave my life to God.

God had plans to use my love of books in a different way. My greatest joy is to witness for my beloved Savior in my writing.

I'm the second oldest in a family of five and share a home with my sister. She's also my best friend. I also enjoy working in my church, gardening, home decorating, and genealogical research. Please visit my

Web page at www.terryfowler.net.

Yours in Christ,
Terry Fowler

The employees of Thorndike Press hope you have enjoyed this Large Print book. All our Thorndike and Wheeler Large Print titles are designed for easy reading, and all our books are made to last. Other Thorndike Press Large Print books are available at your library, through selected bookstores, or directly from us.

For information about titles, please call:

(800) 223-1244

or visit our Web site at:

www.gale.com/thorndike
www.gale.com/wheeler

To share your comments, please write:

Publisher
Thorndike Press
295 Kennedy Memorial Drive
Waterville, ME 04901